SPREE

by

Jonathan DeCoteau

Animus Nor Books

Paperback ISBN: 979-8-9885704-8-6
eBook ISBN: 979-8-9885704-9-3

For God, for family,
and for anyone who has lost a loved one

OTHER BOOKS
BY THE AUTHOR

TABLE OF CONTENTS

TONIGHT:

November 3, 2012

CHAPTER 1

Fay DeSoto (17)—*Fay was just your average high school loser trying to get a life.*
Her friends texted endlessly about her, and she gained and lost weight so much people wondered if she was the "it" girl or the "it" that ate her.
Fay was smart, not really much of a party girl, but Fay was a party girl in training because she was hopelessly desperate. She felt she needed to put on an act to get friends.
And, oh, Fay was an alcoholic—a disease everyone ignored, including her, until it claimed her life and the lives of two other innocent people.

That's what my obituary should have read, though it didn't. It went more like this:

Fay DeSoto (17), *only daughter of Bill and Helen DeSoto, died in a car crash after hitting a caravan late Saturday night. She was a member of the National Honor Society, active in student government, and on the local youth council at her church. Donations may be made to the Burgundy Hill Ambu-lance Association. Funeral arrangements are pending.*

You see, the only thing I really had to look forward to was a party, if you can even call a bunch of wasted kids stumbling around a party. I guess it was the only place where feeling lost suddenly became socially acceptable, where you can stand surrounded by people and still make feeling lonely like something of an art.

It wasn't much, but whatever it was, it was my life—at least until November 3, 2012.

That's the day everyone in town learned my name.

It all started innocently enough—when doesn't it? — for a girl out to get too drunk to remember her life.

Kyla, my girlfriend who always acted like she was terrified of getting pregnant, but never had any reason to worry, told me about this party. I know how superficial and stupid that sounds, but this wasn't just any party. Alex, my ex, was hosting, and rumor was he was going to name his new crush there when all the ladies were assembled. I knew I wasn't going to be the one to get picked—I'd cheated on him months earlier, before he cheated right back on me—but at least I could spread rumors about whatever girl he chose, which would make the night something of a success.

I was the one driving. I know that for sure. I remember having a drinking spree on Heinekens—most of my boyfriends drank them—and didn't think much of it. It took a lot to get a girl of my mass drunk. Not that I was big—just curvy. I remember that Kyla was freaking out and that Mandy, my other girlfriend, the cuter one, the one who didn't have to try too hard to get boys to like her, was too busy applying last-minute makeup to take the wheel. So, even though it was Kyla's car, the honor fell to me. Under most circumstances, I was the best driver of the three, and it would take more than just a few beers to get me too buzzed to drive.

It just so happens that the old beige jeep started bucking, that another car, a green caravan with a mother and her daughter, came just my way at just the wrong time of night. It was pitch black. The latest song from anyone but Katy Perry was blaring, and there was a whole lotta blackness, the kind that swallows nights whole and leaves them for dead.

I wish I could say that I remember more details. But all I remember is singing along to a song I can't remember, seeing Kyla making a funny face to mock my singing, of hearing Mandy go on and on about how she could never apply eyeliner if the jeep kept hitting potholes. I remember this sound that can only be described as pure cacophony. It was a combination of a flash, of sweat, of all the senses rolled into one—that last second before you know the car's about to strike—of blinding thunder, of metal tearing into metal, ingesting it into itself, tearing it apart—the sound of death by DUI.

It was so fast I never even saw the mother's whole face—just the lines of worry, the fading mascara, the eyes so wide they reflected the light of the metal just before the crash. I never saw the daughter—at least, not when I was alive. Believe it or not, Kyla's fat, mocking face was my last sight of life. After that, the cars were too conjoined, like some mythical monster you read about in English class. Kyla was lying still, too still, and Mandy was covered with blood from a slash across her forehead. Her back and legs were pinned. She was crying, unable to move. The daughter was okay—just a few abrasions. The mother—her head went through the windshield. Just after her head tilted just enough to look back, to see that her daughter had braced herself. In death, I recognized the daughter as a girl I went to high school with. I saw my body last of all, maybe because my head wasn't with the rest of me. It was like some horror picture we hooked up over on a Friday night—only it was my severed head, my open blue eyes looking back at me.

I'll never forget that night, out of all the nights I could have died.

And it's not just because that's the night I did die.

It's because that's the night I didn't.

At least, not entirely.

Instead, I woke up, if you can call this waking up, and found that there was still some part of me, some spirit, some soul this lapsed Catholic never believed in, only it couldn't just float up into clouds or go down into fires. It was just there, looking in on the world, in on what was once my body, staring at what was once my life.

I heard the shrill cry of sirens, the vapid hum of spinning tires just before they screeched to the grinding halt that happens on cop shows. The reporters weren't long after. The texts and Twitter posts were immediate.

It was official. I wanted the night I'd remember for the rest of my life. I got it.

I expected to see a world made of light, of endless horizons. I remembered my mother reading it to me once, when I was a little girl and asked her what heaven was like and if Daddy was there. She told me Daddy definitely wasn't. He was just gone. Then I was told there were just balls of light that floated like dandelion seeds in the air, then fell, forming gorgeous white sands by a silt riverbed. Somehow, that's what I thought heaven would be like. As for the other place, I never gave it much thought. I was a good girl. An NHS kid. I'd never need to worry about going there.

But there were no dancing balls of light. No illusions that might please a child. Instead, I got the feeling of being rooted to the earth, as if I just couldn't leave. It wasn't the car. I could levitate above it, see the body that was me from all kinds of perspectives, the head at every angle, showing every displaced black hair. I could look myself in the eyes, see death staring back at me. No, it was something deeper, something more primal, something I couldn't quite define. I was stuck. I could float, move anywhere, with the grace of a single thought, but I couldn't just disappear into time. All I could do was take in the shrieking of sirens, the pounding of hearts, the spectacle that was about to become my legacy.

It was hardest seeing the mother. Her eyes were closed, and blood trickled in her blond hair, making her look that much bloodier. She was so still, with pale skin, taut cheekbones, and a certain beauty in her silence. She looked young. I could almost feel the youth in her skin. Her kid, Steph, who I never knew that well, was pounding against glass, screaming out. Steph survived because of her mother's presence of mind. At Steph's angle, her mother wasn't visible. That gave me a thought: I never prayed much. I never much believed in anything but what I saw with the eyes. But for a moment, a part of me prayed Steph would never see her mother as she was, curled, unable to answer her cries. I went over to touch her cheek, but it was cold, even to the touch of a ghost, which I guess I now was.

"You can't save her," a voice said.

I turned to follow the sound. It was unique, more like a whisper that floated through the voices, the chaos all around me. I watched as a cop called for the Jaws of Life, as Kyla and Mandy were lifted out, unconscious, waiting only for Life Star to arrive. If they woke up, they'd remember this day forever, the day they lost their closest friend. If they didn't, they'd soon be here, standing with me. But not yet. This voice wasn't theirs.

I kept searching through the rushing cops and paramedics. Standing off to the side, with people rushing through him, was a pale teen with dark bangs, a spider tattoo, and a gothic trench coat that might've been cool twenty years ago. Around his neck hung a noose. He looked up. His eyes were vacant, empty of light, just black sockets, black pits for eyes, matching his overall appearance.

"Who are you?" I asked him.

He just looked at me with what would've been eyes, but with what felt like only emptiness.

"You really need to ask?" he inquired.

I thought of whether I'd lost anyone in my family. I hadn't, not since my grandmother, years ago. I half-wished to see her, to have her take my hand. Instead, I was a ghost about to be scared of another ghost.

"Crazy T?" I asked.

"The Butcher of Burgundy Hill in the flesh—or out of it," he said.

He smirked a little. Most people looked better with a little smile. This kid looked morose. I could imagine why. News accounts had it that he'd shot two kids dead at school before taking his own life. He was said to be found in the woods by the high school at the end of a rope with two smoking holes in his skull. Rumors of homicide ran rampant. All I remember is hearing about it years ago when I was a tiny kid. He gave me nightmares. Looking at him now, I could see why.

"Are you the local haunt?" I asked him.

"I'm one of them," he told me. "There's more of us than you can imagine."

I knew I wanted to ask him all the big questions of life, the universe, eternity, and if there was something to drink in the afterlife. All I could ask, however, was: "Am I stuck here forever?"

"You are in forever," he told me. "You're one of us."

"But is forever here, this place?"

"It's everything—this place and what comes after."

"What does come after?"

"Hell," he told me. "I'll send you a text—if I get service in hell."

"Why are you here, then?" I asked.

"For your Death Day, of course," he told me. "Who do you think led you here?"

"I don't understand."

"You don't have to," he said. "Not anymore. You should've, though, the time I made sure your friend's beer was stocked, the time I told you where to hide out when you and that worthless friend of yours were out drinking, the time, just before last period, when I made you feel a little thirsty."

I remembered every one of those times; they each came with a tingle.

"I worked so hard on you, since you were a kid," Crazy T said. "You were destined to be one of us. I guess some ghosts just need to learn the hard way."

"Take me away from here," I said.

"I can't," he told me.

"Why?"

"Because it's your Death Day."

"You keep saying that. Why?"

"You only get one—the day you're welcomed to the afterlife. Soon, you'll realize you were always there, anyway, but we still celebrate it. Tradition, I guess."

"Then where's my family? Where's heaven?"

"Every Death Day is different. And yours, well, it isn't going to be a happy one. That's why you get me."

"Why?"

"Because you're one of us now. You're a Taker," he told me. "I knew someone would eventually take my place, but you seemed like such a sweet kid."

In the silence, I felt the people around me moving faster as I grew more apprehensive, slower as I wanted to just step outside of things and take a look. The speeds kept clashing until it became apparent. I was listening to the Jaws of Life tearing the mangled caravan apart to get at the mother and her kid.

"Damn," I said.

I stood watching with Crazy T, like some ghoul out of a Dickens' Christmas story I was forced to read in English class.

"Are you the ghost of Christmas yet to come?" I asked him. "Is this what *might* be?"

"This is what is. You're never going back to this life," he told me. "But on your Death Day, you have to face consequences. The consequences of what you did are just as bad as what I did."

I didn't say anything for a while, just watched as paramedics got at Steph, freed her, tried to shield her from the sight of her mother. The thought shot me across town to where my own mother was lying asleep, still under the pretense that I was sleeping over Mandy's, that I'd wake up the next day and walk through that door. I wanted to wake her, to cry to her for help like I did when I was a kid, but instead I felt pulled back to the crash site, to Steph, to the mother.

"Where's her spirit?" I asked.

"Damned if I know," Crazy T said. "Heaven, maybe. It's the one place I can't see."

I tried to concentrate, to see heaven. Nothing came. Crazy T sensed my frustration. "It'll come in time," he said, "when you learn to be open to The Flow."

"The what?"

"It's The Life Consciousness. It connects time, space, the universe, with feeling, events, people, and places. It'll suck you in when it's your time to go to hell."

"You mean The Force? Just my luck," I said. "I get to spend eternity with a *Star Wars* nerd."

"You'll feel it—in time," he told me. "Just like you'll feel everything your victims felt."

"My victims? It was an accident."

"There are no accidents."

"I didn't kill myself on purpose."

He smirked again—that ugly as hell smirk. "I'm somewhat of an expert on that," he told me. "And I can tell you that you killed yourself and these people just as assuredly as if you shot them with a gun. Trust me. I know."

I grew quiet, just watching as kids from the high school started driving by, some even stopping. The cops talked to each other and agreed to block off the street. I got a glimpse of one of their cells. It was 2:15 a.m. My night was just beginning.

"I didn't mean for any of this to happen," I said.

"But it did," he said, "because of you."

I shut up.

"Don't worry," he said. "There's a place I'm going to take you once this is all done, the place we all go to sooner or later."

"Where's that?"

"Spree."

"What a weird name."

"It's a temporary teenage hell," he told me. "It's the greatest rush you've ever felt, or the greatest nightmare. It calls to the spirits of all the dead kids, and it'll call to you. For judgment."

"Why?"

"Everyone is summoned."

"For what?"

"To be a Keeper or a Taker."

"Taker?"

Crazy T pointed up. I could see these black mists circling around my friends as they were loaded into Life Star, following after the copter as it flew off and away.

"Some help keep life; some take it," he told me. "Depends on how dark the soul. You're a Taker. I can recognize my own kind. That's why I helped you die."

I looked at the holes that were his eyes with aching curiosity.

"I know what you're thinking," he told me. "But I assure you, I'm the sweetest mass murderer you'll ever met. I never shot anyone who didn't deserve it."

"I wish I could say the same," I told him. "What I did—the accident—it killed..."

"*You* killed. But you might hold off on prosecuting yourself. The other Takers will do that for you."

I stood next to him, waiting for the inevitable. All the bodies were gone. Except two. My body and the mothers were covered, put into the only ambulances that were in no rush to speed off. Police were calling for trucks to get rid of the totaled cars, getting workers to clean up the broken glass on the road. Even in Burgundy Hill, open roads were the priority.

"I did this last time, two years ago," one of the officers said. "Why the hell do these kids die on my watch? The one night this week I was asked to work the late beat."

"I'll go with you," the other officer said.

I'd seen them around town, but I never knew them well enough to know their names. The badges read Jameson and Deriega. I felt myself there with them, pulled like a magnet against the cool silver of night, unable to do anything but follow. They talked about what a waste it was, how one of their daughters was in an accident two months ago, but was okay. They went on about what they planned to do with their weekends, and then, as they drove down the familiar streets—White Mountain Road, then South Spring Street—about who would knock and about who would say what.

As they pulled into the driveway, the clock next to the wheel said "3:33." I remember feeling that was ominous, for some reason.

There was a knock at the door. No answer. No one knocks on doors in the respectable town of Burgundy Hill at such an hour. Another knock. Also unanswered. A phone call. A light turned on in my mother's room. I felt her presence, confused, slightly afraid, slightly irritated, but still composed, still peaceful. I'd never quite feel that in her again. She put on her slippers—these old fluffy white ones that blackened over time but that she wouldn't throw out. They were a gift from me four Christmases ago. She made her way to the door, looked out at the windowpane, wondering whether these were real officers and why they were trespassing on her peaceful night.

I closed my eyes as the door opened, as the officers spoke the first words.

"Ms. DeSoto?"

I didn't listen. I just felt the immense surge of anguish, of anger, of confusion that made me first understand the beat of a truly broken heart. The pain was so much I doubled over. I tried to think sweet thoughts of comfort, tried to project images of happiness, of myself as a small baby, of anything that might soothe her pain. But the anguish was too great, an immense flood of red and black that circled around her so much so that even the Takers that hovered around the police were blown off by it. It was like a supernova of the soul. It reminded me of a picture I once saw in art class, an immense painting of pain on a canvas that would never quite come clean.

"I can see it," I said, when I could gather the words. "I can see pain."

"You can see emotions," Crazy T told me, "because you can see the part of hell opening up that gives people those emotions."

"My mother really is in a living hell—because of me?"

"A soul can escape, but it can take years," he told me. "I don't see her escaping anytime soon, if ever. You, I don't see escaping at all."

The anguish swept over me again as my mother asked for just a moment away, as she went to my room, inexplicably, and checked for me, as if this was all a misunderstanding, as if her baby might still be under the covers. I could feel her shock. It was the only thing that matched her agony. She stumbled around, searching for the light, stumbled upon an old beer cap I had forgotten to pick up after Kyla and I had a few drinks in my room last weekend. She felt the odd texture, even underneath her slippers, reached down to pick it up. As the cops called out to her, she clung to the wall, briefly, holding the beer cap in her hand. The time: 3:44.

FIVE DAYS LEFT

CHAPTER 2

I tried to channel this Spree, to cut the misery short, but I felt pulled towards the last place I ever thought I'd spend any of my afterlife.

It was my old school, the Monday morning after my death.

Some kids were crying; some didn't care, shuffling along on their normal day as if no one had died. Everyone was talking about me, Kyla, and Mandy, though, even the teachers. They had been called in for an emergency meeting. They were gossiping about how they thought I'd appeared drunk in class once, but how they said nothing. I smirked. Only once? I'd gone to school drunk dozens of times. Maybe if they had said something, I'd still be alive. Maybe not. I heard Mrs. Walters, my pretty blond English teacher, say: "She was a lost soul." I never knew she felt that way. I thought she was just trying to be nice when she talked to me. Mr. Higgins, my portly science teacher, said that I acted like a little brat in his class, which I suppose was true, and that he felt sorry for me. Mrs. Cowell, who had these giant lips, was the school psychologist, and said that I used to be such a good student, but that I'd skipped a few times and she had been worried.

As the principal marched in, along with crisis counselors and the rest of the school counselors, I could feel the weight on his shoulders. He was Mr. Buckley, a soft-spoken, kind man who genuinely loved kids—just not the gremlins they grew up to become. He had these old-school bifocals, and he tilted them before speaking. He spoke to thank the teachers for coming in early and then laid out the plan for the day. I felt myself pulled somewhere else.

Slumped over a locker in the hallway was Zipper, real name John Chatterly. Everyone called him Zipper because he kept completely to himself and looked a little like the character with the spiky black bangs from the old *Doonesbury* cartoon. He carried this commando style bag he was endlessly sifting through when he wasn't getting bullied. He mingled with other kids well enough, but he was weird. He insisted on being called by his nickname, even by teachers. As he grew older, his demands grew more ridiculous. He once insisted that a picture of a brick wall appear in place of his yearbook photo. I think he just wanted to erase himself out of existence.

I talked to him years ago, when he was closer to normal. He liked me then. I liked him. We were a couple, if middle school couples count as real couples at all. He was my first kiss. It was a little like kissing a fish that had been in the freezer for a while, but it was cute in a middle schooler way. I never thought of him since we broke up, but when I saw him, I thought that he was nice, but bizarre and depressed. He had these three Takers in black cloudy form hovering around him as if he were some kind of ghostly portal. I guess I was number four. His aura was dark, darker than black, with occasional red flare-ups that reminded me of a gigantic black hole we once studied in science class. He had ear buds and was singing out lines from "Angry Johnny" by Poe. He had pictures from the morning paper, pictures of our wrecked car, and had other kids' pictures in the bag, marked with gunsights. One of the pictures was mine. It had no gun markings, though. I wondered how such a psycho could walk the halls freely, but then I remembered that I'd kept away from him, too.

"Don't worry," he said, looking down at the pictures. "I'll get you trending on Twitter."

I could tell that he channeled some of his anger at me. His aura suggested that he was planning something that would make the news. Not necessarily a school shooting in the gun-kids-down-in-the-cafeteria sense, but something just as awful. The weird thing is, he was so close-mouthed, and such a good kid who did what he was told that as obvious as all this was to me, it wasn't obvious to anyone else. I could see a small pistol in his backpack; I could feel him handling it. But no one else ever saw him for what he was. The kid barely kept up on Facebook, unless he was stalking victims. He seldom texted and preferred to keep to a book. He was just a kid off the radar, even his own parents' radar. He walked to school through the woods opposite Sherman Street—watered-down survival training, I suppose—arriving early to print out homework at the school library. As withdrawn as the kid was, he was still smart and got good grades. He could put up a facade. For that reason, he was never in the guidance counselor's office, even though just being around his aura gave me an icky feeling.

I fought my Taker impulses, fought not to add my anger to his own. Something pulled me into the hospital room with Steph—something that felt like anger. She was just regaining consciousness from a night of fitful rest, just being reminded of what happened. I could see her aura—a pink, protective, loving energy with the blackness that now entered because of what I had done. A friend texted her as the friend was arriving at school, wishing her love. I knew that Steph was furious, and rightly so. She knew I'd be mourned and remembered well, that her mother's killer would be cried over that day, while her mother would just be kept in the town's prayers. I felt she was right to hate me. I'd hate myself too.

"Pure anger," Crazy T said. "You gotta love the taste of it."

I didn't know he was still around. I'd felt consumed with my own aura.

"Is it time for Spree?" I asked.

"Not just yet," he told me. "You have a few things you must face first."

I knew what he meant. The school kept calling to me. I could feel myself being drawn to an ocean worth of grief, anger, indignation, loss. There was every emotion I could imagine, even some I couldn't, all swishing together in a huge of sea of negativity. A few waves of red and blue swept through me, before moving on to the next kid.

Mrs. Cowell was busy hanging up these giant sheets of art paper in the halls as the kids gathered around the gym. I sensed that kids were supposed to sign them with a personal message to my mother. The principal, a few crisis counselors, guidance, and a few of the more personable teachers, met the kids and guided them to the gym, as if it was a mile away. I wondered why many came to school at all, but I sensed that they wanted somewhere to meet, to hug, to grieve, in a public way, somewhere away from the cameras of the reporters who were already on site at the school.

"She was such a good friend," Laurie Schmidt, my old friend in band, said.

I wasn't a good friend. We hadn't spoken in years, but I could feel that the tidal wave of emotion had consumed her anyway.

"I yelled at her just before she left," Gretchen Wasoki said.

She hadn't really yelled, just told me she was trying to get to her locker. I'd forgotten the comment as soon as she made it, but I'd never have the chance to tell her so.

Behind the seniors came freshmen, also crying. They knew something had happened, didn't know me personally, but knew of me, and cried out of obligation.

After all these kids I only half-remembered, Alex came walking in. He was too cool for the bus, the star soccer captain who always had a car, even freshman year. He wore black sunglasses that matched his curly black hair, and they just barely managed to cover up his red eyes. He looked taller than I remembered, about six feet, and more muscular, with a spray-on tan. As cheesy as the image looked to me now, I knew he was the only guy I could ever say I loved. I could feel, in the subtle teals and blues that circled around the kid, that he'd loved me too. I could also sense, in the maroons that darkened his overall mood, that he was angry, irate even, at my stupidity, at my infidelity, at my death.

"I'm sorry," Gretchen told him as he walked by.

Alex looked back, said nothing, kept walking on.

He bumped into Zipper, who wasn't watching where he was going. Alex looked at the kid and said nothing.

"Prick," Zipper said and kept walking.

I sensed, in the sudden swirls of green, that Alex didn't take Zipper seriously, that he'd found joy in bullying the kid, in pounding away at the strange and unfamiliar.

"What'd you say?" Alex asked him.

He grabbed Zipper's backpack—the one that had the gun in it—and gave it a shove. Zipper went circling towards the wall. I wanted to make the gun go off, to get people to notice, but I couldn't do a thing. I didn't know how yet.

No one laughed. Everyone knew the tenor of the day.

Zipper murmured, but Alex didn't follow up. He just went up to the paper mural Mrs. Cowell had just finished putting up and picked up one of the markers she'd attached to a string.

I stood over his shoulder, looking on as he wrote:

Hello, Ms. DeSoto:
I'm sorry your daughter was the worst girlfriend ever.

Kids who'd seen him write it stood back as he walked away.

The teachers were too busy congregating with the students, huddling and crying with them, to notice.

Even though my mom would never see the comment, I felt so angry I could slap Alex. He cheated on me too, though after, I admit, I'd cheated on him. Just last Monday we were all lovey- dovey, throwing markers at each other in Mr. Higgins's class. I thought we were moving on.

Today, this.

I saw Alex scamper off, towards a bathroom stall. He locked himself in, pounded on the stall a few times, and then broke down and cried like the kids he made fun of.

I wanted to hold him, but I couldn't.

I just knelt by him and said: "I wish I could undo it all, but I can't. Just know that I love you, too."

Just then, I felt myself pulled elsewhere, up and floating, above the crowds of crying kids huddling off the buses and into the gym, away from the anger, the grief, the accusations.

"What's happening?" I asked.

"Looks like someone's made her Death Day wish," Crazy T said.

His voice sounded uneven. His black hole eyes sparkled in this reddish light of insanity.

"It's no matter," he said. "I want you to see something before we go."

He pointed to the image of Zipper holding my picture.

At that moment, I remembered. Zipper had cried when we broke up in eighth grade. I laughed before heading off to have my first beer in Kyla's basement.

Yeah, I was a real jerk.

"He liked me too much," I said.

"He loved you," Crazy T said, mockingly.

I watched as Zipper stalled himself up in another bathroom, then took the gun out of his backpack.

"Maybe today's the day," he said to himself.

I could tell Alex had humiliated him. I could feel how sensitive he was, could see it in the pink orbs that floated around him. If they only knew how alike they were, they could grieve together. But a world of status and condescension separated them: the world of high school.

"You wanna help?" Crazy T asked me. "You wanna undo it all? Maybe you should've thought of that before you got behind the wheel."

I watched as Crazy T transformed himself into a cloud of blackish mist, like the Takers hovering around Zipper, urging him on.

"Don't do it," I whispered to Zipper. "Forget me. Live. Just live."

I could see Zipper jump up a bit, then calm down and put the gun back into his backpack.

He zipped it up and busted out of the stall, off to his first period class.

Faint whispers of light surrounded me, and I knew I was somewhere else, somewhere that looked a little like the smoky haze of a never-ending party. Around me was music blaring in colors along with silver shadows dancing, spilling into each other, and the smallest hints of gold that framed the whole place in infinite metallic fire. I felt I was in a field, surrounded by creatures I couldn't even make out. Their presence felt unsettling, but familiar.

"Is this hell?" I asked.

I searched around for Crazy T, but I heard no answer.

"Spree," I heard an unfamiliar voice say. "Land of lost souls."

"I can't quite make it out," I said.

"You will—in time," the voice said. "Every teen does."

"Why have I been called here?"

"It was you who called us."

A girl stepped forward, dressed in gothic attire, with painted black eyebrows, empty eyes, nose rings, and burnt black skin. She stepped forth from the song, the music circling around her.

"We lost our names when we lost our lives, but you can call me Burn Girl," she told me. "I'm the oldest of the lost souls. After Crazy T. I like to burn things. Hence the name."

"How nice."

Several more shadows materialized. One looked like a preppy girl with hair-sprayed red curls, ripped jeans, and scabs all around her body. Casting a larger shadow still was a thin male figure hanging from a tree, its neck disjointed.

"This is the land of killers, isn't it?" I asked.

"We've all killed. I set fire to a party I wasn't invited to, killing seven girls," Burn Girl said. "I was never caught until I set a fire so big I couldn't even escape from it."

"And I cut and cut and cut until there was nothing left to cut," the red-haired girl said. "They call me Cut Girl."

"Naturally."

"And I was a bully, sentenced to die the way my victim did," the hanging shadow called out. "I don't have a name."

"We're what you can see and feel of Spree right now," Burn Girl said.

"You're Takers," I insisted.

"We're the Takers who surrounded you when you got into the car, when you drove it, when you crashed, when you were beheaded," Burn Girl told me.

She pointed her singed finger at another apparition. It was me, a corpse with its bloody head in its hands, its eyes staring out into the metallic fire.

"You will join us soon enough," the hanging shadow said. "Every Taker does."

"What exactly is a Taker?"

"Keepers preserve life; we take it," Cut Girl said. "We're drawn to the thrill of killing, of blood," she said. "I can taste your blood—even now."

"Once you see what you've done, you'll join us," the hanging shadow told me. "A Taker must be with other Takers, must feed off of them."

"But first," Burn Girl said, "you made a Death Day wish."

"I have to save the people I've hurt," I replied. "I have to save my friends from ending up dead. I have to stop the school shooting."

"You won't succeed," Burn Girl told me.

"Let me try."

"Your wish will be granted," Burn Girl told me, "but know that we'll be there, watching, and that we'll pick our own Taker to go against you."

"Crazy T," I said.

"It's his special project," Burn Girl told me. "He died killing just two of his classmates. Zipper could be the first school shooter to kill them all."

"Not if I can reason with him."

"You can't."

"Let's wager, then. I lose—I'm all yours."

"You can't barter with what we already have," the hanging shadow told me. "But if you lose, you take whoever Spree tells you to, whenever Spree tells you to. You take Crazy T's place until hell calls you."

"Agreed."

"You have one school week until the shooting," Burn Girl told me. "Five days."

I felt myself pulled away from the parties, from the endless fires of color. I could see the school in the background and right in front of it, the hanging shadow, or Rope Man, as I called him, twisting in the air. Flies swarmed around him, and a smile took his lips as the lunch bell rang and kids with senior lunch privilege leaped through him on their way to their cars.

Later that day, I wandered the halls of the school that I couldn't believe I wanted to save. Crowds of kids huddled and cried, while others were walking and talking, without a care in the world, but too afraid to even smile. Half of these kids spread rumors when I was alive. Now they all bawled like they were my friends. Not one ever said I had a problem drinking. Not a one ever really cared. Yet, they set up a Facebook page in my honor, as if I'd died a saint and not a drunk. Special texts of "Remember Fay" circulated with funny comments I supposedly said. I was never that funny. And then there were the banners. I walked up, right through a couple of kids planning out how they'd cheat on Chemistry homework.

"Fay:
I remember that time I held you on the river by Sue's house. We laughed and talked and nearly fell off the boat. You were my first kiss. I'll treasure you always. –Kade"

I honestly was too drunk at that phase of my life to remember who Kade even was, let alone whether we'd ever kissed.

Another note triggered a memory I'd nearly forgotten:

"You used to call me names, but I forgive you. May we make up in heaven one day. –Dora."

It was true. Dora had dyed her hair blond one year, and it looked horrible. The roots were drenched in black. I laughed, made fun of her, even put my friends up to wearing wigs from the dollar store that looked just like her hairdo. The thought that the moment stayed with her, long after I'd forgotten all about it, saddened me. From where I stood, it seemed like everyone forgets people and remembers moments. A single thought, feeling, or impression stands out, and that's all you are to them. I wonder if anyone knew the real Fay at all.

I floated by the wall for a while before I felt another emotion calling to me. I could see fountains, waves of blue just pouring out from the classroom. The aura was spilling over into other auras, contaminating them with grief. I floated into the room only to see Mrs. Walters, my English teacher, the one who looked a little like Tinker Bell. She was staring out at my former desk. I'd left a book there without knowing it. Mrs. Walters placed it aside in a pile, with my name facing away from the rest of the class. She was rearranging desks, pushing and pulling, trying to get rid of the desk the dead girl sat at. She'd given this thought over the weekend, considered even making a small shrine to my memory, but she opted to switch the room around and to take one flower and put it in a vase with a card next to it, a card dedicated to my memory. Given how many detentions she gave me, most of which I'd earned, I was shocked. I was even more shocked to see her breaking down, to see another, older male teacher come up to her and give her a hug.

"I never lost a student before, not like this," Mrs. Walters said. "The last time I saw her, I was writing her a detention."

It was true. I was late to school that day. I was too consumed with drinking the night before. It's a wonder NHS didn't kick me out ages ago, by I always managed to get my service hours done.

"I know it hurts," Mr. Higgins, my science teacher, told her. "What hurts more is that she won't be the last."

"I don't know if I can take teaching," Mrs. Walters said plainly. "It hurts so much. I felt I should after...well, I felt I could help kids through. Now I'm not so sure. I can't get what happened to Fay out of my mind."

"I had Fay in homeroom," Mr. Higgins told her. "Kids liked her. She was a cute little girl."

That was a lie. I was anything but little.

"But she was only one of my students," Mr. Higgins went on. "Right now, we have to think about the rest. They'll be looking to you for leadership. Be strong."

Mrs. Walters nodded, drying her eyes as Mr. Higgins went back to his room.

Right on cue, the bell rang, and poor Mrs. Walters—she was a newer teacher, so I gave her a hard time—did all she could to maintain her composure. The first student walked in, Jessica Hanson, another one of my former childhood friends who I grew away from. Jessica noticed that Mrs. Walters had been crying. Jessica awkwardly put her books on a desk, not sure which was hers in the new arrangement, no doubt, and came up to Mrs. Walters. She gave Mrs. Walters a hug. More and more kids came in—Tom, Sue, Alex—and they did the same.

Looking on, I was prouder of each of my former friends than I ever was of myself.

And it's not like I hadn't seen them at their worst.

Half those kids bullied each other by text. More than half had bullied me the moment I became known as the local party girl. More than one was a drunk.

But look at what they were capable of.

Look at what this school could do.

This was something real. This was something worth fighting for.

Zipper sat commiserating with the band kids.

The kids were all gathered in the cafeteria for a special lunch paid for by the school.

Zipper talked about how he remembered me from my middle school days, about how we dated. He looked almost like he belonged as part of the group. I could see his aura—all red and black—intensely hateful, intensely angry. How well he covered it up with smiles as he went on about the one teacher who still gave homework on a day like this. You always heard about school shooters being freaks, outsiders in trench coats, victims of severe bullying and abuse. But Zipper acted just like a normal kid, looked like a normal kid, but wasn't at all as right in the head as the other kids were—if there is such a thing as a teen who isn't crazy.

As the kids talked on, his aura darkened even more. He was contemplating what it would be like to go home and kill the small squirrel he'd caught and tortured in his basement. He wanted to know what another life's blood felt like splattering his hands. As preparation. He'd planned to do this right after his Pre-Calc. homework each night until the shooting. He had hoped the formulas wouldn't take too long. And no one noticed. Just from the intensity of his aura, I could tell he was thinking about it over and over, to the point of obsessing. Yet, he sat there, not missing a beat in the conversation.

Minutes later, he politely dismissed himself, went outside, ostensibly to throw out his lunch and take in the crisp fall air. He looked in every direction. No one else was around. He took out his gun from his bag, looked into the cafeteria. No one was looking. There was a rush, a thrilling red vibe that took over the colors swirling around him.

"Not just yet," he told himself, fantasizing.

He called out a name, maybe Alex's, and shot the gun at a small rock. He smiled. Kids came rushing out. By that time, the gun and the smile were away.

"What the hell was that?" Tom, who'd just comforted Mrs. Walters earlier in the day, asked.

"Trash got in my way," Zipper said, walking past the trash can, back into the cafeteria. "It won't next time. That I promise you."

The principal closed out the day before the cameras, addressing the entire community with a monotone befitting an administrator. His eyes made it to the reporters, but not to the half-drunken kids who could hide their addiction better than I could or to the blossoming school shooter who sat surrounded by acquaintances he called friends.

"Fay Marie DeSoto was one of the most popular and ambitious girls I've ever had the opportunity to meet," Principal Buckley said, "and we all miss her dearly."

As he droned on, I wondered if he even remembered who I was.

"To lose a girl this young, in such a way as this, it hurts us all," he said, adjusting his bifocals. "We constantly ask ourselves why we had to lose Fay at all, why Kyla and Mandy lie comatose, but all we're left with is their absence and with each other. Fay loved this school."

Really? *Loved?* Even in the afterlife, I didn't know what he was smoking.

"She loved her friends, and she loved the support she found here," Principal Buckley went on. "Her friends will recover, and we will help them. We're a good community. We're a strong community, and we will pull through this, no matter how long it takes. Because Fay is with us, a part of us, and her smile will live on forever in the halls of Burgundy Hill High School."

That part alone sounded more like a nightmare—a fate worse than replacing Crazy T.

"We want parents to know that qualified counselors have been working with their kids throughout the day and will be available throughout the week," Principal Buckley said. "The faculty and staff thank all those who have reached out to us in this time of need, all the other schools who've offered counseling services. We in the Burgundy Hill High School family are determined to make sure that Fay's life will send a powerful message to other students and speak to the need for responsible behavior. And we will stand by Mandy's and Kyla's sides, no matter how long their recovery takes. We ask now that reporters respect the privacy of students, faculty, and parents. We direct all reporters to speak to Dr. Irene Richards, our superintendent of schools."

The cameras flashed, the questions flew, and token friends I wasn't even close to circulated, talking to reporters just outside the school about how awful they were feeling.

I shook my head as I watched the reporters pounce like locusts on unsuspecting kids. They devoured every tear, every frown on the face of a child, billing it as exclusive content for the six o'clock news.

I watched as the principal concluded the service with a brief ceremony. A tree with a small plaque above it was planted in my honor. Cameras flashed, and I wondered if these pictures would make the front page of tomorrow's papers or just the local news section. Despite all the grandstanding of grief, I felt touched by the show. It's just too bad a kid has to die to be remembered.

FOUR DAYS TO GO

CHAPTER 3

An image of a lost, pale kid with hazel eyes and disheveled long black bangs came into view. I didn't know why. I sensed the kid was packing his bag when his father came into view. His father was a drinker, and watching the old man down the whiskey, then scratch a wart, ignited something in the boy. I felt the boy's fury, not because his father beat him—maybe because his father didn't even care enough to do so. Instead, this balding, lanky middle-aged guy ordered the kid off before the man grabbed the paper and lounged in a ratty recliner with plaid, seventy-style upholstery, still drinking. I sensed the man didn't have a job. And I could tell the boy lost respect for the man, realized that the man was legitimately hurt in a construction accident, but had been sponging off of insurance money for the past two years. In that time, his wife had left him, and the man had turned to alcohol. This boy felt so alone.

The boy scurried off, leaving his father behind, but not before going to the gun case and jimmying the lock. The man was a hunter, a real man's man before he became a drunk, and he had all kinds of hunting rifles, knives, and gear. The boy took only two guns—one a rifle of some kind, the other a pistol. He also took a vest and a hunting knife before searching around for some rope. After he found it in the garage, he came back. I saw him look at the man as the man prepared to watch *Good*

Morning, America. The boy's eyes became slits; they looked so vacant, like they weren't even there. The boy stepped forward with the hunting rifle and then muttered about not wanting to risk it. He packed the pistol in his vest pocket, placed a smaller rifle and rope in his bag, and headed to school. It was much later than he should've been going, and I sensed that he was waiting for something. As the kid's thoughts clarified themselves to me in his aura, I could tell that he was waiting for gym class, third position. All the kids he wanted to kill would be there.

I tried to talk to the ghost, to tell him not to do this, to beg him. Clearly, I'd missed out on the real killer. I felt so sure. But maybe it wasn't Zipper. Maybe it was this kid all along.

The more I tried to talk to the kid, the more I saw that he was determined to go it alone.

A small yellow SUV, the kind my mother once drove, pulled over. I saw a younger version of my mother get out. Her maternal instincts had taken over. She sensed something was off, but felt sorry for the kid.

"Hi, Teddy," she said.

"Hi, Mrs. DeSoto," he said in reply.

It hit me. I stopped trying to intervene.

"Just watch," a vaguely familiar voice told me.

I did. This was the day Crazy T blew away two jocks at the school. I forgot what it was like before the shooting. We lived on the same street. Everyone knew of everyone else in so small a town. Even I knew who Teddy was, and I was only five. He had played with me once or twice at Ocean's Edge Park. I had fun, even giggled. I looked up to the older kids. I even looked up to him.

"We're headed into town," Mom said. "Would you like a lift?"

"Thank you, but I'm all set," Crazy T told her.

"Shouldn't you be in school?" Mom asked.

"Who are you, my mother?" Crazy T asked her.

His voice was snotty. He pulled his hand towards his vest pocket.

"I'm sorry," Mom said. There was an awkward silence, and she added: "I just thought you looked sick. I thought I could help."

Crazy T kept his hand on the pocket.

"I am sick," he said. "But before you know it, I'll be fine."

"Suit yourself," my mother said. "Just watch out for traffic."

"I know, Ms. Desoto. Have a nice day."

"You too."

"I will."

I saw Mom go back to the jeep. A little girl, me at a younger age, stared back with her pale blue eyes. She waved to Crazy T, and Crazy T waved back. We then drove off. My mother told me to be kind to Crazy T and said that he didn't have a mommy anymore. The concept baffled me, but I knew that I was supposed to be nice the next time I saw him. I never got the chance.

As Mom talked to me in the car, Crazy T headed to the small woods near the school. He found a great big oak. It was one that had special meaning to him. He had played by it as a kid. On Friday nights, though, the area became one of the teen hangouts, mainly for getting drunk. I'd gone there a few times myself not long before I died. I knew that Crazy T had been invited to a party, told that a girl he liked named Lisa would be there. I knew that two kids had gotten him drunk just to beat him up. He was an ugly kid—not athletic, smart, or social, and no threat to them. Just an easy target: a kid without friends trying to make some. They'd beaten him up there, ostensibly over the way he looked at some girl, and thrown him against the tree. He lied, drunk and unconscious, until morning. His father never even noticed that he was gone.

The rope he now tied against the lowest sturdy branch he could find wasn't for him. It was for them. In fact, he cut the rope and formed two nooses, not just one. He didn't want to kill them quickly, just get them to run into the woods and have fun with them. He'd pick them off one at a time. Crazy T fantasized about shooting at them as their bodies jerked and twitched at the end of the rope. I saw him approach, put on his vest, take out his rifle, and strap his knife to his belt. He made sure he had the rifle ready and started looking for a position to lodge himself as a sniper between the gym class and the school. I felt his breathing grow heavier. I could hear the kids playing soccer rushing from one goal post to another as Crazy T found a secure branch on the edge of a second tree. He'd fire a few shots from there, then run back to the tree with the nooses. From there, he could corral a few of the kids into the woods where his real fun began. I could see so many Takers swirling around both Crazy T and the soccer players that the sky looked as black as a moonless night.

Crazy T positioned himself, aimed his rifle.

"Closer," Crazy T whispered. "Just a little closer."

Birds began to grow frantic. A few sparrows, rustled from the branches, took flight.

The fleeing birds and a speck of piercing sunlight peeking through the clouds gave away Crazy T. I saw a player point over to his direction, laughing, until the first shot rang out.

The gym class didn't know what to do. Many continued playing ball until a second shot rang out and one of Crazy T's tormentors crashed to the field, half of his head blown open. The players screamed, boys and girls alike, some covered in blood, frantically dashing in all directions.

Crazy T shot repeatedly, but his breathing was heavy, and he felt rushed. He hit one girl in the leg and fired a sniper bullet into his second tormentor's back. The boy dropped dead, unaware of who had killed him or of why he'd died. Takers lifted the fallen boy's soul up, devouring it until it too was as black as night. Bits of light gathered around Crazy T, fighting with the Takers. I couldn't make out their faces, but I sensed they were Keepers doing their best to keep the Takers at bay. The Takers flew off, feverishly trying to cling to any boy or girl, to bring the extra targets into Crazy T's line of vision. But just then the Keepers rustled a few more birds that flew out, startled, over Crazy T. The birds striking his gun and shoulder upset his balance, and Crazy T fell. In that moment, a Keeper whispered to the girl shot in the leg. I saw her reach for her phone, dial or text something. Crazy T approached the team, firing away on the remaining members. He was too flustered, though, and lost his aim. Unintentionally, he wounded rather than killed. The kids played dead. The girl stopped texting, but the phone was pointed towards the woods. It was the distraction that saved lives.

Crazy T put the phone in his sights and fired away. As Crazy T took his shots, giggling, a soccer player who had gone around the school and back to the woods knocked the rifle out of the shooter's hand. Crazy T stared with a blank white expression. He was caught totally off guard. The boy, a stocky, flat-faced guy with a crew cut, wrestled Crazy T to the ground. Crazy T reached for the knife on his belt. The two fought over the knife until Crazy T was able to stab the kid in the leg and run away. I'd never seen anyone run as fast as Crazy T did, back into the woods, mud and dirt and stone flying up all around him. The player called out to his friends, a few who were just behind him, and made pursuit. Injured as he was, the boy couldn't catch up with Crazy T. His friends were still too far away. The boy grabbed the fallen rifle. Crazy T took out his pistol and fired some shots, but the boy looked like he knew how to handle a gun. He shot back, and Crazy T dropped the pistol and focused on running.

Crazy T made it back to the tree with the noose. Shots rang out around him. Crazy T climbed the tree as quickly as he could. He put one noose around his neck. The boy with the stab wound came through the woods just in time to see a twisted smile on Crazy T's face, the one I saw when he first appeared to me. Crazy T fell with all his weight, instantly snapping his neck. The boy took two shots, both of which landed in Crazy T's skull, but the school shooter's fate was already certain. Dozens of Takers seized Crazy T's soul, a shade of pure black, and yanked it from his body. They circled around him, devouring him, until the entire flock of Takers disappeared. The Keepers gravitated around the young hero, until police showed up, combing the woods. My last vision of the day was the body of Crazy T still swinging, helped along by a gentle breeze.

I shuddered. Just then I realized that I was seeing the last few seconds through a YouTube video entitled "The Butcher of Burgundy Hill". I saw the angle shift until I made out the face of the boy looking on admiringly, until I saw the smile on the face of Zipper.

It was strange.

Zipper's home life was hardly the wreck I thought it must have been.

He was a quiet kid, but he could talk and make friends when he wanted to.

His parents checked in on him, asked him how his day was, and then trusted him to complete homework in his room.

He was an NHS kid, the kind who had a real future.

Like me.

Only tonight he was in his room alone, researching school shootings. There was a song playing, one that might have been by Coldplay, if I remember correctly, and a list of shootings longer than such an obscene list had any right to be. It was about the history of American school shootings. Some were famous, like the Bath School Disaster, where Andrew Kehoe, a local treasurer, handyman, and farmer, set off three explosions, one of which was in an elementary school. It was said that he was angry over an increase in property taxes that led to foreclosure on his farm, so he planted petrol in the school for a year while performing maintenance on it. One morning, he killed his wife, set his barn on fire, and while firefighters were tending to the barn fire, ignited the school, full as it was of little kids. Kids flew everywhere. Kehoe eventually killed off his superintendent, among others, with a bomb that blew Kehoe up too.

The history was a long one, and not just in the last ten or twenty years. From what Zipper was researching, school violence had been with us always, with episodes of teachers killing teachers and even some kids, with episodes of students open firing on other students, and one case where Native Americans scalped a class of kids in the colonial era. Gangs factored in, for at least seventy years, and decades before that, some kids actually were allowed to bring weapons to school. We were a nation founded on violence, and it ran like a red, bloody streak through the history of our schools.

Zipper studied each case intelligently, and I could feel the conflict in his thoughts. Should he shoot so soon after my death? Should he wait? Wouldn't he get caught? He wasn't sure. Zipper had a picture of me, one he kissed repeatedly. I realized that he imagined my voice talking to him, that he heard me telling him to avenge my death.

He whispered, "I'll see you shortly, honey," then kept surfing the Net.

I barely knew this kid. I went out with him a long time ago, yet he seemed to have this image of me that he worshiped, an image in stark contrast to the teen drunk that I became. If Zipper ever went to the parties I went to, I'm sure he would've been cured of me real fast. But now it was too late. He was singing along, researching soccer games. I shook my head. It hit me. It was nearing the twelve-year anniversary of Crazy T's attempted killing spree. And unbeknownst to the athletic director, he had scheduled a Class M championship soccer game the very night of the anniversary of the shooting, right in the same soccer fields. Zipper was going to make history by repeating it. He was going to beat Crazy T's count, try to kill more than anyone ever had in a school shooting.

Zipper blasted the music louder, started typing a personal blog message he intended to post on Facebook, Snapchat, and Twitter just before the game.

"To all my so-called friends:

See you in hell.

-Zipper"

I tried to think of a happy memory, of some small joy I might send this kid—any thought I might give him so that he'd let go of the hate. But all I could think of was when we once laughed and splashed as kids at the local pool. I whispered reminders to him as he typed away, but a great darkness swept over him, and I could sense that the other Takers were standing in the way.

"Not to worry," Crazy T told me. "You'll see your boyfriend soon enough."

I could see Crazy T and the Takers surrounding me, could feel their darkness calling to the darkness within me. But there was one light I didn't let go of—my love for my friends. I clung to that image of light even in the midst of the consuming darkness. I felt like I was suffocating in the all the hatred and negativity, as if the life was literally being sucked from me into a greater black hole of Takers. I fought, struggled to free myself, when a being of pure light pulled me from the devouring flock of Takers.

I looked up and saw myself surrounded by light, tiny phosphorescent gold and silver orbs. They circled the sun before one broke off and settled on a form in the woods. The form that was taken was of Belinda Tallimere, a small girl from our class who had died of cancer when she was just a young girl. It was her voice I heard earlier. It was she who must have granted me the vision of Crazy T's killing spree. I remembered vaguely playing recess with her. She had the best laugh; it sounded like wind chimes caught in a summer breeze. Now I saw her again, running as a little girl, before she appeared, looking quite beautiful, with blond hair and green eyes, like she would look if she were my age the day I died.

"Belinda?" I asked.

She nodded.

"I thought for sure you'd be in heaven."

"I will be," she said in her sweet little voice, "when I grow up."

I realized that the spirits of children made up The Keepers. They grew up and spiritually matured before taking the long walk to heaven.

"You're not as I remember you, Fay."

I looked at myself; so much shadow stood over me, swallowing what was once human. My head was gone, held in my hands. Shadow mixed with only the faint sparkle of light in my eyes. My body was more mist than mass.

"I'm a Taker, aren't I?" I asked. "I'm going to hell, aren't I?"

Belinda's ghost walked among the woods she used to play in as a child. She didn't answer me directly, but instead picked a few azaleas, smelled their petals. She was beauty in motion. I watched, saw, actual music in her steps. Her movement was like a symphony. The other orbs gravitated towards her, giving her almost an aureole-like glow. She looked just like an angel from a Renaissance painting we saw in art class—just more luminous.

"You're still so pretty," I told her.

She smiled. Belinda always loved compliments—before she lost her hair.

"You stopped coming to visit me in the hospital," she said.

It was true. A group of us, Kyla and Mandy included, saw her when her illness became somewhat of a fad in the school. Whoever brought the best gifts to Belinda earned social status in our school; whoever had a video of the encounter earned more. It was like going to see a teenaged Buddha or something. But when the fad passed, so did my interest. No kid wanted to be around a kid that was sure to die. It reminded me of the rather inconvenient truth of my own mortality.

"I'm sorry," I told her. "I was too...selfish."

"Too drunk is more like it," she told me.

I didn't deny it—though I would've had to be a very young drunk at that point. Just saying.

"But in death there is only sobriety," she told me. "There are no drunks in hell, only those who feel every tongue of flame. And there are no drinking parties in heaven—just those who feel the ecstasy of God's love."

"I wouldn't know."

"But you can know—that's why I'm here. You're the one I've been waiting for before I go to heaven."

I nodded, though I was confused.

"I loved my classmates," she told me, "and I was sworn to watch over them. I am their Keeper, and I've chosen you to be their champion."

"But I'm a Taker."

She touched me, told me to listen.

I heard a hundred laughs, cries, thoughts rushing through me, the laughs of my classmates.

"I didn't know Tom had a crush on Kyla," I said.

Belinda giggled.

"Other Takers can't feel what you feel," she told me. "And Keepers can't see the darkness you gravitate towards in Zipper."

"So I'm neither. But Crazy T told me—"

"Crazy T has been working to make you a Taker since he died."

"Why me?"

Belinda waved her hand. An image of Zipper staring at me on a middle school field came up.

My friends noticed, rolled their eyes, and whispered. I was too busy looking some other way.

"My death set off Zipper," I said plainly enough.

"It will—next Friday."

"So that's when the five days are up. That's soon. I thought I might have one more day."

"The Takers want you to think that. They want you to lose," she said.

I thought for a moment. "My alcoholism. Did Crazy T plant that on me too?" I asked.

Belinda looked sad for a moment. Her light diminished ever so slightly. "Crazy T only influenced you to make the wrong choices so that he could use you to get revenge, to finish the job that he started," she stated. "You made the choices yourself. You alone are responsible, and you will find your place in the afterlife based upon who you were and what you do now."

"There's a chance I may not go to hell?" I asked.

"There's a chance you may save your classmates, my classmates," she said. "That's all you need to concern yourself with."

"But how?" I asked. "Crazy T has so much more power. I have none."

"You'll find the power when the time is right," Belinda told me. "And my Keepers and I will stand with you. You will not fight the last battle alone."

"There's no time for me to find the power. I need the power *now*."

"It's the afterlife, Fay. There's time enough for everything."

Belinda started shrinking, transforming into a butterfly of pure white light, then into an orb.

"I'm sorry I wasn't at your funeral," I told her.

"Then make it up to me. Make sure no one else in our class has one this week."

I nodded until the light blurred. I was left standing alone, with neither light nor darkness, by an old oak within the empty woods.

THREE DAYS LEFT

CHAPTER 4

Hours before my funeral, the kids went in to a bit of a surprise.

It was lunch. Outside the cafeteria, Steph, the girl who's mother I killed, was there, standing, staring at the murals that had been covered with well-wishes for my friends and me. She still bore the abrasions from the crash. Hundreds of signatures, of comments like "We're pulling for you," or "It could've been any of us," infuriated her. The red and black swirled in her aura. I could sense the colors building in her, all around her, in a storm of activity. Steph went up to the first covered wall and tore violently at the paper. She took the pages signed by my closest friends first, reducing them to pieces and spitting on the pieces as she hurled them to the floor.

The gesture angered Sue, one of my old drinking buddies, who happened to be heading to the bathroom in the middle of Steph's tirade. Sue ran up to Steph, fought to restrain her, before a counselor and some teachers on lunch duty came out to see what was up. By the time Sue confronted Steph, nearly half the hallway was strewn with little pieces of paper and decorated in saliva. A crowd of kids came to watch as Sue tried to reason with Steph. Steph just pushed Sue to the floor and cursed.

"She was my mother," Steph screamed to the kids massing outside the cafeteria. "Your drunk friends killed my mother!"

Steph broke down; a few kids rushed to comfort her.

"Where were her flowers and cards?" Steph hollered, sounding almost animalistic in her high-pitched screams. "Walls and walls for the drunk! Not a single signature for the life she took!"

The counselor and teacher stood there, letting Steph scream out what was inside her.

"Damn you all," Steph screamed. "You're all guilty!"

She stormed off. The counselor stood at a safe distance, waving the teachers off.

"Give her time," the counselor said. "I'll go see that she's okay."

In the corner of the crowd stood Zipper, watching the pieces of my life on the ground, covered in spit. I saw him squint at Steph, take in her image. As I stood there, bawling over what I'd caused, he just looked at the girl. Cold. Detached. I knew that he'd just added her to his list.

I hadn't checked in on my mother since the night of my death. I don't know if some moments have the power to age you years, but that's how my mother looked. Aged beyond her years. I knew from her aura that just hours before she'd been crying, huddling over albums of me as a pink-ribboned baby, looking in my room at night, reminding herself that it all really happened, that I was really dead. She sat next to a collage of my life, with pictures of me as a tiny, freckled girl playing jump rope, to pictures of me at the Cape with my friends surrounding her. She looked like she could barely stand.

And now here she was, surrounded by kids, one fine afternoon when her only daughter was to be laid to rest.

I always wondered what kind of funeral I might have one day when I was old. I imagined I'd be surrounded by my kids and grandkids, that I'd be elderly and wrinkled from all the life I left behind me. I never thought drinking would kill me. I never once thought I'd die before twenty-one. I used to sing "If I Die Young" by The Band Perry on nights when I'd binged, but it was just a song, not a prophecy. Yet, here I was, with a hundred sobbing kids, cameras, and a town mayor paying honor to the life of a little drunk who never should've died.

I scanned the audience as the mayor was photographed paying respects to my mother. Alex and Sue were there together. Alex was expressionless, still hiding behind glasses, but his aura was dark, the color of leaves just before they fall in winter. And he felt just as cold. I knew he was still in shock and that staring up at a closed casket didn't exactly help him come to terms with the fact that I was gone, that he'd never hold me again.

Hordes of girls crowded around after kneeling before my casket, pretending to pray, and then paying their respects to my mother. Some bawled. Others simply went through the motions for the dead girl in the class. They talked about me, not all in flattering terms. One girl gossiped to her friend, calling me a slur at my own funeral and said I'd brought it all on the town and on myself. I couldn't disagree with her on the second point. Others criticized me for cheating on a guy as cute as Alex. I couldn't answer that, either, only that I was searching, looking beyond me, beyond drink even, for something that wasn't there. I was confused, and I took it out on Alex.

But today, I spent most of my time trying to hold my mother, to let her know that I was still there. She was the one whose aura was half depleted by the enormous pain I'd caused her. She barely responded to my estranged father, a drinker himself, as they spent a moment crying together. I held her hand, but I knew she couldn't feel it. I told her again and again how sorry I was, but I knew she couldn't hear my words.

"Is there some way to get through to her, some way to let her know I'm okay?" I asked.

For once, I hoped Belinda was around me with some kind of sage advice.

There was no answer, but I felt myself concentrating on a picture. There were so many on a few posters, from me as a baby at the hospital, to me as a toddler, to me getting ready for the junior prom, my black bangs specially curled and full of barrettes for the occasion. I saw myself in shorts running along the beach at the Cape and as a middle school on a whale watch, laughing with my friends as we spotted a hunchback whale far off of port. Finally, there was the picture of the dress I wore for prom, white linen with cream-colored lace, a beautiful dress for a beautiful occasion. But perhaps the moment that touched me the most was the moment my mother pushed me after I got my training wheels off my first pink bike. I felt so proud, with the wind whizzing behind me, like I could go anywhere. On the back of the picture, I remember writing, years later: "You'll always be my wind and because of you I'll always fly." I concentrated as hard as I could until the picture blew towards my mother. The mayor was still paying respects when the picture fell upside down at my mom's feet.

Somewhere across town, another casket was made ready for a funeral that would happen only hours after mine. This was where more cameras were set up, where the mayor had to be as he bade my mother goodbye. This would be the funeral for Steph's mom. A good number of kids planned to attend both funerals, but not all. Not my friends.

My mother looked as the kids started heading out, saw the small photo at her feet.

"I wonder how this got here," she said, reaching down, picking up the photo.

She saw the message. Through her tears, I saw a faint smile.

It was the one smile that made all the pictures of all the events I ever attended worth it.

I watched as the people left me there, as it was just my casket and me. Only the tail ends of sad auras remained behind.

"It's funny how quickly people move on," I said. "I died less than a week ago, and already some kids have forgotten me."

"But others never will," Belinda replied.

I thought back; it was true. Some girls in our class never were the same after Belinda's death.

"I hope they do," I said.

"I hope not," Belinda said. "If you are forgotten, it will be because a greater tragedy takes hold of the town."

I felt myself flying, moving through time, space, objects at light speed. The entire town became jumbled images until I saw myself walking down a winding patch of White Mountain Road.

"What is this?" I asked Belinda.

Ghouls seemed to be simply appearing out of these portals as if this was a massive undead airport. They looked around. Some had black faces or eyes, like Crazy T, the telltale sign of a Taker. Others had light outlining their body, glowing through their eyes, the sure sign of a Keeper. There must have been at least fifty spirits appearing right on White

Mountain Road, as runners jogged through them, cars whipped by, and the trees blew in the only sign of the natural world that something out of the ordinary was afoot. Most never even acknowledged my presence.

"This is going to be the most spiritually active place on earth in three days," Belinda told me, "as the forces of Spree fight for control over what may turn out to be the biggest school shooting in history."

"Why do they care?" I asked, simply enough.

"To be a Keeper is to care. It's how the souls of children and teens grow enough to see the full merits of heaven," she told me. "After this event, whatever happens, some Keepers will move on into eternity."

"But the Takers. Why try to kill? Why care?"

"Takers can't kill," Belinda told me. "They can only take dark souls to Spree and influence souls and events with their dark energy. Once they grow dark enough, they'll disappear into hell, but to gain favor in hell, they'll take as many kids with them as they can."

I watched as the Takers and Keepers kept pouring in, so much so there was a spirit floating around every other foot or so.

"I have to stop them," I said.

"You can stop nothing," Belinda said. "You can only influence. Every soul has autonomy in Spree."

"Can I at least see Spree before the end?" I asked, "as part of my education. We all know where I'm going, anyway."

I heard just a note from Spree, a chiming of ocean waters, wind, and sands, and felt myself standing on the sea. I looked around me and swore I saw this giant golden tree that I thought of as the Tree of Life. I knew that every soul came from here, that every soul would come back through here on its way to eternity. I felt enveloped by waters that reached up and wrapped themselves in light around me. Flowers sang, music engrossed the air, which was as elemental in its beauty as the earth. My thoughts gravitated towards one figure in light: Alex. I pictured Alex and me hugging, standing on the ocean, by the great tree, the light of our souls intertwining and mixing as if we were one soul. But just as quickly as the image was shaped, it was gone.

I saw another figure standing on the water, wrapped completely in light. She had a graceful, sloping cheekbone, eyes of perfect blue, and hair that was a light, burning fire. She had just come from heaven. I knew immediately who she was. I opened my lips to apologize, but I heard, rather than saw, her speak.

"Save my daughter's life," her voice said to me.

And with that, my vision of Spree was gone.

A vision of Zipper standing over Steph, blood still dripping from her skull, haunted me instead.

"Help me," I said to Belinda.

"You've just had your most important lesson," she told me.

The image of Steph extended until I saw the entire school flooding with blood, Takers everywhere, at least fifty kids shot dead. I saw the bodies piled up, the shooter hanging on the same tree Crazy T killed himself on years back. Parents lined the parking lot, blocked off by police as they cried out to determine whether their children were among the living or the dead.

"That's the Takers' vision," she told me. "It threatens to swallow Spree whole."

"I'll do whatever it takes," I said.

Belinda looked at me, no longer the cancer-stricken girl I remembered, but the confident young woman she would have become.

"Remember that when the time comes," she told me. "The Takers are coming for you. Be strong."

She waved her hands, and I was gone, drawn towards the hospital, where two Takers were gambling for the lives of my friends.

CHAPTER 5

"Time's run out," Rope Man, one of the darkest Takers, taunted.

Kyla was over on a white bed, with only the faintest hints of respiration. Mandy didn't look much better. I reached over and touched Kyla's hand. I could feel her soul rising and standing beside me. It was a misty black, not unlike mine.

"Where am I?" Kyla asked me.

The other Taker, Burn Girl, taunted me as well, telling Kyla: "With the girl who took your life."

I attempted to ask Belinda for guidance in communicating with the living, but I couldn't feel her presence, her protection. It was just two Takers and me, surrounded as we were by darkness.

"I can't see anyone, anything," Kyla said.

I saw the blackness eating at the light of her aura. She panicked, as I had done.

"Because you're not dead," I told her.

She stared at me, at the blackness that was my body, at my decapitated head, weighing me.

"Fay?" she asked. "Is that you?"

I felt her fear as she looked at what was left of the face of an old friend.

"I'm dead," I told her. "The accident killed me."

Kyla started crying, bawling, feeling guilty, prattling on about how she should've driven her own jeep.

"It's not your fault," I told her. "It's mine."

"Believe her," Burn Girl said. "If you'd been driving, you'd all still be alive."

"Don't listen to them," I told Kyla. "They aren't your friends."

"And you are?" Kyla asked me. "Look at me!"

She looked at her lifeless, pale skin, at her limp black hair, at the black mist around her, unable to reconcile what she was seeing now with what she saw on the bed.

"How could you do this to me?" she asked. "I trusted you. You were my best friend!"

"There's more," Rope Man said to her, "much more."

Burn Girl came forward, a spiral of red, jagged burn marks wrapped up in blackness.

"You know Tom, your first love," Burn Girl told her. She smiled a bloody smile as she spoke. "You have his child inside you."

"No," Kyla said.

She thought back. With the darkness so near me, the Taker in me could see her thoughts before me. She realized that she hadn't taken anything before the accident. The child had been detected by doctors, had been growing inside of her all of these weeks.

She looked at me the way a child does at a betrayer.

"Listen to me," I told her.

"How could you do this to me?" she asked.

"Tom, the whole school—they're all in danger," I told her. "If you help me—"

"Help you?!"

"Don't listen to her," Burn Girl said. "What good did she ever do you? Listen to us. We're offering you a way out, a way of togetherness, a new life."

Burn Girl waved her hand and a vision of parties, of sensuality, of fast cars, of no consequences, emerged before her. Tom was in the center, more handsome than others. Even Alex was there, all doting on her. I winced at the sight. It was such a lie.

"These Takers mean to drag you straight to hell," I screamed. "Kyla, listen to me. Think of your baby!"

She was lost to me, wrapped up in their lies, in the blackness that surrounded them, invisible even to my undead eyes.

"It's still not too late," a third voice said to me.

It was Crazy T, emerging as he did from the blackness shared between Burn Girl and Rope Man.

"You can't deny yourself forever," Burn Girl said.

"But I can deny you," I told her. "I won't let you take me or my friends."

"Try to stop us," Crazy T challenged.

I fought to call up an image of Spree, of love, of the one thing that might drive away these Takers from my friends. Burn Girl just laughed, calling up supernatural fire and thrusting it at me. I felt the burn, the scorching, the melting even, of my skin. I curled up, wailing, trying to protect myself. I called out for Belinda, for a Keeper anywhere, but no one came. It then occurred to me, in all that pain: The fire had control only if I let it. It was Burn Girl's plague, not mine.

"How did it feel?" I asked her, rising to my feet. I felt my Taker energies. I used them. "How did it feel when your own fire surrounded you," I asked, "the moment you knew you were about to die, that no one would save you, that no one wanted to?"

Burn Girl's fire recoiled, tangled itself around her, but it did not burn her.

"Your friends will find out," she answered.

"We mean to finish the job we started," Rope Man added.

"And when your other friend comes around enough to emerge, we'll take her too," Crazy T promised.

I could feel my anger. Anything loud, fast, uncontrollable felt subject to my whims. Suddenly, I felt like I had a budding control over objects after all. Like a little poltergeist, I thrust the metal knives in the room towards the three Takers. The metal went through them. They stood unphased.

"You're learning," Burn Girl told me. "Soon you'll be with us, right in time for the shooting, right in time for all of us to go to hell together."

The image of me walking forward, head in hand, again stood there, mocking me.

I tried to cover Mandy, to protect her, but the black and red mists that were these lost souls only circled around and disappeared before I realized that doctors were rushing in, through me, fighting to save Kyla. As I looked on, helpless, Kyla flatlined.

I fought to control my thoughts, to stand guard over Mandy, to warn her, but I felt pulled, almost against my control, to school, where the darkest energies in town began congregating. I felt so uncontrollably angry. I wanted to torment every Taker I came on then and there.

"Easy," Belinda's voice told me.

She was so light I couldn't see her through my darkness, only feel a little more composure and hear her sweet, still childlike voice ringing in my ears.

"They took Kyla," I told her. "How could you stand by and do nothing?"

"Your friend made her choice," she told me. "She always was a Taker."

"Tell me how to grow stronger, how to get Kyla back," I insisted.

"You can't," she said. "They're about to announce her passing over the intercom."

"So why am I here?"

"To save the school from a Taker invasion," she told me. "First, you have to see what they're going to do to this school if they get their way."

The announcement over the intercom, right in the middle of lunch announcements, may not have been the best way to handle Kyla's passing. Kids who just had to cope with the ordeal of one kid and one parent passing put their heads on their desks, silently crying. Others, fueled by their anger, started making careless remarks. One of the angry girls was Steph, fresh off her mother's funeral. I saw how expressionless her face was the moment Kyla's death was announced. She waited until she was in the lunch line between classes. Two of the girls in my circle of friends were behind her.

"At least two of the girls got justice," she said, loud enough for Sue and Jessica to hear her.

Sue was closer to Kyla than she was to me, and I could tell she became Steph's target in the absence of any other whipping girls.

Sue stood for a moment and then said, "Say another word, and it will be your last."

Steph stopped, tray in hand. "Going to finish what your drunk friends started?" she asked. "Careful. You'll have to walk in a straight line to get to me."

Sue smacked Steph across the face. Steph grabbed some hot sauce and splashed it across Sue's face, wetting her makeup and smudging it that much more.

"What's the matter?" Steph asked, mushing more sauce into Sue's face. "Can't keep anything down without some booze? Don't worry. You can throw it up later. Isn't that what you do?"

Sue pushed back, knocking Steph out of the line, just into the cafeteria. The kids got a good, quick look before the girls were on the ground, pounding away at each other. Throngs of Takers surrounded the girls, suggesting punches to throw, fueling the anger of the girls that much more. Friends of both girls jumped in to pull them off, but the girls took a few punches themselves and before I knew it, brawls were breaking out across the cafeteria. Anything from mashed potatoes to spaghetti was flying from wall to wall. I'd never seen kids go from grieving to angry in just moments, but the fight proved that the old cliques still existed in our school.

In one small corner of the fight stood Zipper, expressionless as someone's chicken pot pie smashed him in his face. A few kids laughed, inappropriate as it was with everything going down. Zipper just watched them. The moment they turned to the next carnival sideshow in the food fight, Zipper came up behind one guy and stabbed him with a fork. I saw Crazy T appear to Zipper and egg him on. Zipper stabbed so fast I didn't even catch it. The kid, a friend of Alex's, turned around, stunned, but did not see Zipper there, only the fork in his leg.

"Stop Crazy T," Belinda told me.

"How?"

"Think of what you know of him, of what he's really hurting over. Force him to face it on the final day."

I thought of Crazy T's father, half drunk, on the sofa the day Crazy T killed two kids. I created the image as vividly as I could in my mind, down to the last shade of pale.

As I did, I could see Crazy T at work, whispering, then yelling towards Zipper as he sensed the Keepers floating nearby.

"Grab the gun," Crazy T said. "Shoot! Kill them all!"

I could see Zipper standing there, contemplating.

"Now, send the image to his aura," Belinda called out. "Hurry!"

"How?" I asked.

"Just keep thinking that your thoughts become his thoughts."

I chanted it, even, "My thoughts are your thoughts," until Crazy T saw not a counselor before him, but his father, yelling at him, threatening to beat him again. The memory sent Crazy T flying towards his fellow Takers, away from Zipper.

"Not yet," Zipper said.

By this time, counselors, teachers on lunch duty, and administrators had closed off the cafeteria and were pulling students into corners, yelling at them to stop. Flights of Keepers surrounded the kids, fighting the Takers and repelling a few. The kids appeared to calm down, if only slightly. A new wave of crying, cursing, and sobbing swept through the cafeteria. The school resource officer appeared, calling it in. It was the first time a food fight in our school warranted police involvement. If the police knew how close they came to a much larger issue, I wonder if they would've searched kids' bags and found Zipper's gun. I tried to create the thought, to send it, but nothing worked.

My last sight was a bawling Steph being escorted out of the cafeteria by a counselor.

The Takers had won the day.

Zipper's home was filled with pictures of him as a smiling boy. In one, he stood holding up a bass caught on his line. In another, he won second place in a race when he was ten. In still another photo, he was a player at a soccer middle school challenge and earned a small cup. It was hard to believe what Zipper had become. I sometimes asked myself why, and I wasn't the only one who noticed the change. Sometime around middle school, Zipper grew darker, more depressed. The smiling pictures vanished, and the light in his eyes just wasn't there. It was like he was playing a role for his family, the role of the dutiful student athlete.

The real Zipper had issues, and he was about to take out those issues on a small squirrel he trapped in his basement. I could hear the squirrel sounding out in its animalistic cries, but Zipper was home alone, and he didn't intend for the squirrel to be alive long enough to concern his parents. In fact, he had a whole section of the basement sealed off by a concrete wall that looked like his room. He'd stashed away a few guns, and even had the remains of a few animals he'd used as target practice but had not yet discarded.

I wondered what happened to this kid who appeared so normal. He still called and texted a few friends, but only for cover. Otherwise, he'd just fallen off the face of the earth. Then I saw part of what did it. Zipper had been an early boyfriend of mine, if you can call it that, before I moved into the more popular crowd and started dating guys like Alex. Zipper hated Alex for it. I never knew this. I never saw his naked aura, which brewed into a steamy black every time he took out this picture he'd taken of me and Alex together, kissing, by the school door. I was wearing Alex's varsity jacket and his ring. Zipper felt pain, excruciating pain, over this, and he was unable to get over it. With my death, his pain only became more permanent. Zipper had never failed at anything he'd tried—except getting the object of his affections: me. And now his failure would last a lifetime. He couldn't live with such a failure. Neither could the high school world, as he saw it.

"We'll be together soon enough," he whispered to the picture. "I wish I got to dance with you at prom just once."

I'd heard him say this before. I attempted to flood his mind with moments from the pictures I saw, but it was no use. I attempted to remind him of a memory I'd long forgotten, when he and I talked one day about what we'd be when we grew older. Zipper wanted to be a doctor, after he became the first man to land on a planet outside of the solar system. A man had to have priorities. I wanted to be a teacher after I became a world famous rock star. A girl had to have something to live for. We held hands, if briefly. But even then, Zipper and his obsession with me creeped me out. I broke it off a few weeks later. I assumed Zipper had long forgotten me, had long retreated into his post-apocalyptic world. I was wrong, and the school might pay for it. I sent as many images of light, of love, as I could, but the light couldn't penetrate the Takers that swirled all about him. I was a Taker trying to do a Keeper's job.

"Did you really think I'd let you near my star pupil?" Crazy T asked me. "I've been waiting for just the right kid at just the right time. Do you know he'll kill one kid I just couldn't kill before I died? He'll kill the brother of another."

Crazy T smiled, too lost to the darkness that swirled around him to do anything but feed off of my fear. I knew I was going about it all wrong. I needed to find whatever was hurting Crazy T. I needed to help him move on, or at least to stunt him. I sensed, given the power I showed last time, that there was something about the girl the bullying was over that I needed to discover. But I couldn't figure it out by watching his black hole of an aura.

"Tomorrow's his practice day," Crazy T said, pointing at the pictures.

There was everyone from Alex and Tom to Sue and Steph, the recent addition. I sensed that these, along with two coaches, were the sacred six. These had to die before he killed himself.

"Choose one," Crazy T said.

"One what?" I asked.

"Choose one that you want to save. Alex, maybe?"

His smile grew darker than a starless night.

"That's all you'll get, if you're lucky. I don't think my boy's ambitious enough. With the plan I show him tomorrow, he'll make a clean sweep."

My fear fed Crazy T; I fought to control it.

"Watch my protégé at work," Crazy T added.

Crazy T and the other Takers swirled about Zipper until he picked up a gun, until he saw the squirrel in his sights.

"Slowly," I heard Crazy T whisper. "You can't grow startled. You must learn control."

Zipper shot at the squirrel. It was a direct hit and a bloody mess. Zipper didn't smile, didn't react, as the squirrel cried out, scared for its very life. The Takers kept control, ordering him to extinguish the innocent animal's life.

I couldn't watch, but I heard the trigger. The squirrel cried out again until Keepers swarmed around the innocent life and brought it to its end. I saw the animal spirit rise, join the spirits all around it, as the lifeless body stayed behind. But still, the Takers weren't through. Zipper fired again. His expression didn't change. Not once.

Zipper simply picked up the body and threw it with the other dead animal bodies in a bag. He took it outside, deep into the woods behind his house, to bury. Zipper had a pit just full of animals. He threw it in there, covered it with dirt and leaves. No neighbors were around to notice. He went back into the basement, hid his gun, wiped up the blood. Zipper was still cleaning the blood when his mother pulled in and called down, "I brought McDonald's. Get up here before it goes cold."

"Cold," Crazy T said. "I don't think my man minds the cold."

"In a minute, Mom," Zipper called up. "I'm almost done."

He kissed my photo, put it and his target photos away, and started scampering up the stairs like an eager child.

The phone rang again, and again my mother ignored it. The machine took over, and I heard a woman say, "We're Burgundy Hill Mothers against Drinking and Driving and we're calling to express our sympathies. We go around to any school that will have us, speaking for free about what drinking did to the lives of our children. We're not calling to ask you to join us there, but to join other grieving mothers who went through what you're going through now. We tried to visit, but no one answered the door. If you want to talk, please call me, Louise Chenning, at 860-659-4354. We're meeting after the boys' soccer game at my house on 234 Gold Hill Street at 8 this Friday night. Hope to see you there."

My mother stared at the phone, reached out for it at one point in the message, but did not pick up. She sat alone, a divorced parent surrounded by flowers and cards from people who meant well but didn't know anything my mother was going through. My death had launched her into a personal hell of second guessing herself. She asked questions like: *Didn't I know Fay had a drinking problem? Did I allow her too much freedom? Why wasn't I monitoring her Snapchat and Twitter accounts? Why didn't I ask her to text me from wherever she was, on the hour, after nine p.m. Why didn't I get more strict about who she could hang out with and where she could go?*

Mom imagined the day over again. She imagined herself telling me that I had to come home directly after school, that there would be no parties that night or over the weekend until my grades were up so as not to endanger my NHS status. She imagined that her words would've made a difference, as if I wouldn't have found a way to coax her or sneak out anyway.

Mom had it hard. My father left when we were little. If I wanted to, I could fly to him, see him sitting in a bar somewhere, watching a game with his friends. But he was my father in title only. Mom had worked hard to provide for me after he left. While she had a steady string of boyfriends, she never trusted a man enough to settle down and remarry. Now, in the middle of the worst tragedy of her life, my mother was alone.

I teared up myself seeing her cry. How hard it had to be to sacrifice so much for a daughter who became a drunk like her father and didn't appreciate all the hard work. Years and years of saving up, scrounging, getting by, all for a daughter who'd be dead before her eighteenth birthday. What a terrible waste it all felt like. Yet, I knew my mother loved me and wouldn't have traded me for anything, any more than I might have traded the daughter I'd never have for anything. Believe it or not, I felt the ability to look into the future that might have been. I saw myself grown up, working odd jobs for low wages, all to put my daughter through school after I got divorced. I would've had a hard life, but at least I would've had a life. Instead, I traded my future daughter's life for alcohol without even knowing it. Maybe she would've been the one to break the cycle, to be the professional woman my mother strived to be, the woman I should've been working to be.

My mother got up, canvassed my room for alcohol, found a few beer bottles left underneath the underwear in my dresser drawer. I wasn't exactly careful. And my mother did choose to turn away. She told herself it was a teen phase like the one she went through and that, like her, I'd get over it.

I saw her looking over the mess of clothes I left behind when choosing what to wear the night I died. She broke down again. I went to cradle her, to send her aura positive energy, but that's when Belinda appeared, looking anything but sympathetic.

"Help my mother," I said to her.

She shook her ghostly head. Her hair, thin strands of pure light, cascaded.

"The Takers are confusing you," she said. "Remember your mission."

I felt pure energy glistening all around Belinda, like when the sun gets too bright and spills the extra light across the top of a mountain.

"These next two days will take you down some difficult paths," a voice in the light told me. "But hold strong. Share whatever love you have with the image you're shown, no matter how harrowing, and we will guide you on. We will help your mother, but don't forget your friends. Don't forget the school."

I didn't judge myself as harshly as I should have or fall into a sea of self-loathing. I simply hugged my mother, prayed for her, gave her aura whatever love I had, and let go.

As I did, I could see my mother reaching for the phone, dialing a number, saying hello.

Soccer was huge at my school, where we'd won more Class M division titles than in any other sport, even basketball. And this year we were even bigger. The party I was going to was meant to celebrate a victory in the finals. Burgundy Hill had advanced and was now going after a state championship. The team hadn't played a game since my death, and while I wasn't arrogant enough to believe for a moment that my life or death meant anything to most of those on the soccer field, my death did mean something to one of its star players: Alex.

Alex, a captain, was the team striker and was practicing a few step over moves with his starter, Tom. I'd never really been into soccer, which was practically sacrilege in our town. Watching the footwork between the two as they alternated step-over strategies with one another, however, I couldn't help but admire the skill it took to dominate the ball and your opponent. Everything about soccer was teamwork, and to have a striker with anything on his mind but goals was to invite defeat.

"Stop stepping too fast," Tom told Alex.

"Sorry," Alex said.

Tom looked down. His face had my name written all over it, but he didn't say *Fay*, not once.

"I'm sorry for how it all turned out," Tom said, "and I know today's fight at lunch got you down. But we have to pull through for both of them."

"I know," Alex whispered.

"This is the state championship. We've been waiting for the chance to lead the team since freshman year, and I'm not about to let four years of work—"

"I know," Alex said louder, nearly yelling. "I heard you the first time."

"It's screwed up," Tom said. "This should be the biggest moment of high school for us both, and all we can think about is, well—"

"I won't let it get in the way of Friday's game."

They drilled again, this time alternating the ball, doing something with the forwards that they called the outside foot hook and reverse. Alex messed up the drill, and Tom came to a stop, shaking his head.

"We'll try again," Tom said.

"Later," Alex said. "I need some water."

Coach Ryan stood and watched, muted by the events at hand. Normally, he'd scream up one side of Alex and down the other, but he had a daughter who was friends with Kyla, and I sensed from the blue pervading his aura that even he was a bit down.

Alex stumbled towards a water cooler lying on the side of the field. A few kids hanging out in the bleachers called out to him.

"Hey, man, we need to talk about the party after the game," one kid said.

"We got three full kegs," the kid's friend called out.

They laughed, and Alex nodded, his eyes on a kid standing on the side of the field. It was Zipper, dressed in a groundskeeper uniform. That was his after-school job. Alex stood up, water in hand, and looked at Zipper while he imbibed the water.

"Hey, joining the team?" Alex called out. "You can start by picking this up."

He threw his cup towards Zipper. The two soccer groupies laughed, taken with the excitement of the upcoming game. It was so huge that it was the only time I could remember when the players would dismissed from class early just to warm up.

Zipper said, "No need to get jumpy. Just celebrating an anniversary."

He then disappeared.

"You have a girlfriend?" Alex asked.

By that time, Zipper was far gone, but the groupies still had a good laugh at his expense.

It began to occur to me what Zipper meant. The day after tomorrow was the same day Crazy T shot up the gym class. Judging from his aura, Alex's thoughts were too much on the game and on me for him to get it. That's how much our town tried to the put the past behind us. But one kid hadn't, and even though he was showing the warning signs, walking into the school with concealed weapons, no one was noticing.

Two full days from today, Crazy T and his protégé would have the perfect opportunity. Everyone was going to the game. Everyone. Brothers and sisters of the team, making a special trip from work or college—some of the very kids Crazy T set out to kill years earlier. That year they'd come close to the title, but lost in the finals to Franklin Shore. Now their brothers and sisters would have their chance to become high school legends, and Crazy T would have his shot at immortality. Seeing the Takers circling around Zipper, Alex, and the two groupies, I realized that everyone going to the game didn't mean everyone would be leaving the game without stretchers and body bags. But how to warn them when soccer was the only thing on their minds?

TWO DAYS TO GO

CHAPTER 6

Two mornings before the school shooting, Takers hovered, watching over me.

I could feel Kyla's macabre presence, could smell the fire and brimstone before I could see her.

The memories of my drinking days came back to me.

I saw myself, at thirteen, in the basement, experimenting with cigarettes and alcohol, nothing too big. By that age, at least one-third of the kids I knew had experimented with actual drugs. I wanted to be cool. I wanted to be popular. I wanted, most of all, to be Alex Maroshe's girlfriend. The sweet taste of whiskey intrigued me. Heinekens repulsed me at that age, but I drank them anyway. I found that I could loosen up more if I drank, that I could do more wild things that kids in my class would remember after the weekend was done. As plain old Fay, I was the smart girl trying to be pretty and popular. As Fay the partier, I was uninhibited, wild, and free.

Ironically, I'd just gotten done working on a history project with my ex, Zipper, still John at that point. He'd tried to get me to stay, but I'd run off after mocking him a bit. That's how eighth graders can be, I guess. Immature and mean. As I sat there, surrounded by bottles in a competition to see who could drink the most, I didn't even remember Zipper. Like everyone else, I'd come to forget him.

"Hey, Fay," Kyla told me. "Bet I can drink you under."

I laughed. "Make it worth my while and I'll take you on," I said.

Kyla looked right at Alex.

"Winner gets a kiss," Kyla said to Alex.

Alex smirked.

"So long as you don't barf in my mouth," he said.

"No promises," Kyla said.

We pulled ourselves up to the coffee table. Kids surrounded us, chanted.

"Whoever downs the most in two minutes," she said.

"You're on."

We set up a whole row of scotch, whiskey, Heinekens, Budweisers, even a few light drinks.

Alex called time, and we were guzzling. I saw myself for what I was, a kid, really, who looked ridiculous with foam from beer running down her cheeks. I looked like a mess. I was already bad at applying makeup, but the beer foam made it run even more. Camera phones flashed as kids threatened to put up pics on Snapchat and YouTube. I kept drinking.

Kyla was a true friend that day. She had the weight advantage and could've easily held more liquor than me, but she let me win.

I smiled, looking as awful as I did, and Alex puckered up. I went in strong. That kiss signaled the first time we'd become a couple. Not that it was me, really. It was Popular Fay, the girl who knew how to have fun at parties. Watching my old self kiss Alex, I wondered when I lost sight of who I really was.

The focus changed to an image of Zipper, or John, as he was then, back at his home. He was curled up on his bed, listening to old music from Joy Division, crying his eyes out. He had a middle school yearbook picture of me, and for all intents and purposes, that picture was his girl-friend. He kept it with him always. I felt shame. I knew I had hurt him. I liked Alex, but I never really gave John a chance. There was just some-thing about him—too serious, too depressive, too quiet, too far removed from the friends I'd soon call my drinking buddies.

"You did this," I heard a voice say. "You took my life."

It was bodiless, deep, hollow, but still had some girlish familiarity. The ghostly voice was Kyla's.

"You liked Alex too?" I asked.

I could see her red and blue aura in the vision. She was such a good friend, but still jealous.

"I gave him up for you, and this is how you repay me?"

"I drove that night as a favor to you," I said.

"You did it because you couldn't get to the party fast enough so that you could put down the one girl Alex was going to announce as his girl-friend. You always were so petty."

I looked more closely at what was left of Kyla. She was a giant black mist, not unlike my lower body, but she had this storm above her. Her aura was full of red and black clouds swirling with occasional bursts of gold that looked like pure anger, pure lightning. Her face was sunken in, and her lips and her eyes were black.

"You were going to be the new girlfriend," I said. "Kyla, I'm so sorry."

"No, not yet," Kyla told me. "But you will be."

Kyla threw her storm of anger towards me. I could feel her anger en-veloping me, making me flashback to the time I kissed another boy, Tom, Alex's friend. Alex never burst in and caught us in the act, but rumors started and those rumors were enough to end our relationship. I saw my-self looking up Alex's Facebook status, seeing it change. I saw an image of myself handing him his ring back, telling him that he was making the biggest mistake of his life, that he'd be sorry. Turns out that it was the second biggest mistake of mine.

I fought my way back to the moment.

I was a Taker, I told myself, *and Kyla's exploiting my grief.*

"I don't want to hurt you," I told her.

"A little late for that," she said.

Kyla again threw her storm clouds at me, and again I saw a painful memory, one where she was watching as Alex and I kissed, as we got to talking one summer day. It was by the town beach, and Kyla had just left. I thought we were alone. I was talking to Alex about finding a guy for Kyla.

"That's a hard one," Alex said. "Don't know if I have any friends with arms long enough to wrap around that big a body."

I slapped him playfully, but Kyla heard, broke down as she fled.

The image jolted me back to the present.

"Kyla," I said. "Why in the world would you want to go out with a guy after he said that about you?"

"Because I loved him," she said, "and I wouldn't have run around on him like you did. I would've been the best girlfriend he ever had."

"But you were pregnant."

"I would've taken care of that."

"And killed an innocent life?" I asked. I paused, taking in the coldness of her words. "You're my friend, and I love you," I told her, "but right now, the entire school is in jeopardy. We can fight later. We have work to do now."

The storm clouds of her aura swelled up again.

"Let them all die," Kyla said.

There was a loud crack, like thunder, as her anger and grief mixed, igniting one another.

The Taker in me felt, was drawn towards, her pain. An image of Alex as he was now appeared, packing his sports bag for the last practice before the big game. His mind wasn't on his cleats or his soccer jersey. It was on me. He was still in shock. So much of the school was. But as Alex thought back to the times we kissed, his aura showed no thoughts of Kyla, of his would-have-been girlfriend. He had been using her to get back at me. I hurt him deeply in our on-again, off-again love. He never forgave me for cheating on him, and he blamed me deeply. He wanted me to hurt me like he hurt, and Kyla was the way. This infuriated her to no end.

"Don't worry," she said, flashing me a smirk evil enough to rival Crazy T's. "I'll take care of Alex. Burn Girl and Crazy T promised him to me. I'll be the one who makes sure Zipper shoots him, who makes sure he goes straight to hell."

"Kyla, these are your friends we're talking about here, people you grew up with, who—"

"People who used me, who will get used," she told me. "My life won't be the only one cut short. I won't be robbed out of my whole life by you and do nothing. No, I'll hurt you worse than you hurt me by taking the one person you love the most."

"Kyla," I whispered. "Don't do this. Let me save you!"

"I don't want to be saved."

"But I can help—"

"Save yourself, if you can. Your time to save me passed," she said. "Maybe you should've been thinking of that instead of drinking and driving."

"I *am* sorry."

"I'll make sure of that."

"Kyla, don't!"

"See you in hell," she told me.

I felt her fire and brimstone stench fade, her clouds dissipate, swallowed as they were into a black hole of Taker energy.

Just when I thought it couldn't get any darker, an image of a teen girl wrapped in light stood up, floated closer. Though she was a ball of light and stardust, I could tell, through the well-defined, angular cheekbones, the gently sloping nose, the blue eyes.

"Mandy," I said.

"Where am I?" she asked. "And what happened to your head?"

A cloud of Keepers surrounded her with their balls of light and white energy. They came around me too, keeping me from following my instincts, from following Kyla into the black abyss.

"I need your help," I told her. "I've been killed."

"Is this heaven?" she asked.

"Not exactly..."

My mind flashed to the moment Alex saw Zipper on the field, asked him if he'd joined the team. I got a sick feeling then, and now I knew why. I saw in Zipper's aura what I didn't see earlier, what I didn't notice until my Taker energy was attracted to his. There was an image of Zipper with a shovel, digging by the stands. He'd taken a job as a part-time caretaker around the school with just this purpose in mind. His guidance counselor pushed for it, hoping to get Zipper an opportunity to help pay for college. Zipper was just under the stands, around their supporting beams. He had bought some type of explosive, and he was burying it by the stands. He'd been putting dynamite, petrol, and other explosives under the school grounds, all across the field, under and down along the stands, for months, just as soon as boys' soccer got on a roll. There was enough there to blow up anybody and everybody who had a seat, to blow out the lights, to blow out the field and any players who were on it. He even placed some underneath torn patches in the parking lot, which it was his job to clean up and report on. Apparently, his studies of Andrew Kehoe had not gone to waste.

Zipper played "Adam's Song" by Blink 182 on his phone, played it over and over again, as it was rumored to be the song Crazy T played just before he walked the streets for the school. Crazy T was hovering around him, making sure each detail was right. I knew this was what the Takers were doing, covering for Crazy T so that he could make sure he masterminded everything to perfection. I fought to see more, to see into Zipper's aura, into his plan, into the exact time and place he'd fire his first shot, but it was already too dark. Before I could finish seeing the vision, I felt a light tap on my shoulder and turned around.

"...What happened to you?" Mandy asked me.

"I was pulled somewhere," I told her.

"Why?"

I attempted to show Mandy a vision of the darkness that was Zipper and Zipper's plan, but she didn't see. She appeared unlike any other soul I'd seen before. She'd start out as a radiant light and then diminish.

I put my head on. It would stay in place for only a few moments, a painful reminder of my death to all who came upon my ghost.

"You're not dead," I told her. "You ended up in a coma."

"For how long?"

"Less than a week," I told her. "I died Saturday night."

"If I'm not dead, why am I here?" she asked.

"You're here to stop a killer," I said.

"What?"

"One of our classmates snapped. He plans to shoot the school at the soccer championship," I said. "You've heard of him. Zipper."

"Zipper would never do that," she said.

I tried to call the images I'd seen before, of bodies lying bloodied, of devastated bleachers. None of it made it through the light protecting Mandy.

"This is a dream, isn't it?" she asked.

"More like an out-of-body experience," I said.

Mandy flew up and down, laughed giddily as she flew colorful circles around me.

"Mandy, this is important for you to remember," I said. "You're going to wake up again. I know it."

"Why would I ever want to leave this?" she asked, flying loops around the light.

"Here you're neither living nor dead."

"So how do you know you aren't in a coma?"

"Because I saw my head looking back at me," I told her.

Mandy slowed down in her flying, landed by me. Her smile vanished. She looked at me.

"You're not human," she said. "You're part mist."

"Whatever I was like when I died, that's what I am here," I told her. "I'm something called a Taker. I take lives."

"Not mine?" she asked.

"No," I told her.

Mandy came over and hugged me. "I'm so sorry," she said. "I should've been the one driving."

"I was meant to die," I told her. "It's a long story. All I need you to know right now is that you have to tell people what I've told you about Zipper. You have to speak until they listen."

"Who will listen to me?"

"Alex," I told her, "and Tom and maybe Steph."

Mandy nodded.

"And Zipper. Try to get through to him before he does what he does."

"How?"

"Tell him that I'll save a dance at prom for him," I said. "Tell him that I was with him, that I heard, that I'll be there. Tell him that I promise."

Mandy looked at the swirling black and white mist that was half my body, at the empty eyes.

"I'm not going to see you again, am I?" she asked.

I hugged her.

"Fay, I don't want you to die," she said, in between a few sobs.

I kissed Mandy's forehead.

"It's too late for that," I told her. "Besides, they planted a tree. You can visit me there, if it grows. But first, you need to help me. You need to remember what I told you."

"I'll try."

Mandy began to disappear again, fading into the white light.

"Fay," she called back.

"Yes?"

"What's the afterlife like?"

"There is a heaven and a hell," I told her. "There's just two groups of teens and kids waiting to get to one or the other."

"Are you going to heaven now?" she asked me.

"That spot goes to you," I said.

We waved at each other. I smiled faintly at the beautiful light of heaven that Mandy would one day become. Then she vanished.

Back in her room, Mandy lied perfectly still.

She looked so peaceful for a girl who was flatlining.

Nurses swarmed around her, checking her respiration, her tubes, her injuries to see if there was anything that could be done. I heard them calling for a doctor frantically when nothing worked.

And then, just as quickly as the commotion began, Mandy was there again. I saw her fingers twitch and her ribs rise and fall.

The machines went silent, except for the occasional beep attesting to the fact that life was still there.

The doctor arrived too late, but checked Mandy, probing each wound, determining that she had a crisis but that she was back now and that she should be fine. He assigned a nurse to watch Mandy's room and Mandy's room only for the next few hours. That was more than the hospital, skeletal as it was in its staffing, could afford, but the doctor made the attempt, anyway. I sensed from the blue and gold orbs circling around in his aura that he had a daughter about her age, that he was reacting as much as a father as he was as a physician. I was the happier for it.

When everyone went back to their normal duties, and only one nurse kept watch, ever so briefly, I went up to Mandy's bed. I looked down at her beautifully curved face, at her closed eyes, at the beads of sweat that formed in her fingers. She was such a beautiful girl to nearly die. I always thought she was too vain, too into her looks, but seeing her aura, I realized that she was the best of us all. Kyla always was jealous and hedonistic, and I was always insecure and rebellious. Mandy went along, and maybe that was her greatest sin. But she was still a kind soul. She deserved her life.

I reached down and stroked her hair, gently, the way a mother would. I'd never know what it would be like to be a mother, but I felt protective of my friend.

"Rest, Mandy," I told her, "but not too long. As soon as you awake, tell your friends. Tell Zipper. Tell everyone...if you remember."

I enjoyed the moment with my friend until I sensed the blackness of a Taker in the room.

"You're not taking her," I told the ghost before he could form.

"We won't have to," a voice said.

I recognized the bizarre, uneven pitch that was Crazy T's voice.

He materialized just enough to point down at Mandy's folder on the edge of her bed.

I couldn't grab material things too easily yet, but Crazy T could. He lifted up the folder and stood right next to me. He opened right up to a page where the doctor noted a break in her spinal column. She was being prepped for major surgery, but the prognosis was clear. Mandy would never walk again.

Crazy T smirked, which looked even eerier in the black pits of his eyes. He threw the papers on the floor.

"It's your choice," he said, pointing to Kyla, who hovered around Mandy. "Either your school or your friend."

Crazy T disappeared, and it was just Kyla and me.

I could hear her voice, whispering to Mandy that she was nothing, that she'd be in a chair for life, that it was my fault, that death was wonderful, that she should come along for a safer ride.

"Be strong," I told Mandy.

"She will be," Belinda said.

The Keeper appeared as a blinding, protective light, one not even Kyla could look directly into. Fellow Keepers swarmed around Mandy, showing her images of herself with children, of herself leading a different, but meaningful life. The images gave her life; they gave her strength.

CHAPTER 7

Angry at the attack on Mandy, I lashed out.

The Taker in me gravitated towards the fields, towards the explosives, the deaths that were sure to abound there. The fields were a massive, pulsing black sun calling to all Takers, to all lost souls that fed on fear, death, and hatred.

Even by night, the fields were surrounded by Takers, some I hadn't even seen before. Rope Man was there, a hanging shadow leering out. Burn Girl was there, waiting to stir up new fires, new burns. But there was a group of boys without faces, just shadowy scabs standing guard. I tried to read their auras, but they were too abysmally black. The only picture I could get was of gang wars decades earlier. These were dark sentinels, street soldiers hastening their arrival in hell.

I stood before them, concentrating, seeing if I could picture an explosive, set it off—anything to warn the town. I could feel a small spark of fire forming when I felt a smack that sent me flying clear across the sky.

Crazy T appeared, taller than I'd ever seen him, feeding off of the energy of the Takers. They gave him their hatred, their rage and strength, and he wasn't about to let a slight obstacle like a dead girl stand in the way of hell.

"You just never learn," he said to me.

"So teach me," I challenged.

My hatred only fed Crazy T, who grew powerful enough to send me flying from the field. Flocks of Takers fed on me, magnifying my worst fears. I could see bits and pieces of my classmates raining all around me, overcome as I was by endless Taker negativity.

"I gave you this life, and I can take it away," Crazy T told me.

"You said it yourself," I told him. "I'm a Taker. Before this is done, you'll see that it's me who has come to take you."

I lunged at Crazy T. He became a tornado of energy, ripping me apart with images of my crying mother, of Mandy, paralyzed, of Steph taking a stone to the head in the explosion and dying before being consumed by fire.

In that moment, as Crazy T came for me, I sensed something behind his anger, something that fueled him. There was a face, a girl, who Crazy T adored. The master was more like his protégé than I imagined. I sensed the girl, now a woman, was still alive, married, and close, and anger towards this fueled Crazy T's storm of supernatural activity.

I knew she was still in town, still drawing in the manic energy of this lord of Takers. I'd have to find her, find a way for her to come. Her life, with all the others, might be the only way to shock Crazy T, to get him to relinquish some of his power.

Or it may have been what Crazy T counted on all along.

Crazy T sensed my vision and blindsided me with a barrage of dark energy, flinging one nightmare after another until I fell at his feet. I saw my mother dying, broken-hearted, alone, her final thoughts of me as she passed away. I saw Alex turning to promiscuity, getting closer to other women to fill the void he'd never fill in my absence. I stood up, shaking off the nightmares.

"They're untrue," I said. "You can't lie to a Taker and expect to get away with it."

"Can't I? You really think you know me?" Crazy T asked.

His face became distorted, black, like shadows falling into shadows of greater darkness.

"Bring your friend to me, and I promise you I'll kill her," he said. "Just like I will you."

"You can't kill what's already dead."

"We'll see about that," he said. "Ever feel death coming over you a second time?"

Crazy T started conjuring massive winds of black, the essence of his fellow Takers. The pain I'd caused others, the agony of my head, severed from my body, overtook me, and I knelt for mercy. Just as I fell, Crazy T sent the negative energy right at Zipper until the rage consumed him, propelled him on. The idea was brutal in its simplicity: shoot Alex first.

I regained my strength just enough to fly off, but I wasn't fast enough. The other Takers surrounded me, until I was forced to join their collective, until I felt that I was losing my spiritual body.

"Consider this your punishment," Crazy T told me. "You can stay and watch us take souls until you act like a real Taker."

I fought, but the more angry I became, the more the anger consumed me, the tougher the bonds became. I was trapped, bodiless, in The Flow, and the only emotions I knew how to feel were the very ones that held me in bondage.

Deep inside The Flow, no Keepers could pull me to safety. I felt surrounded by Takers on all sides, seeing their memories, feeling their emotions, consumed by the same rage. There were no faces, no names, nothing but a collective of negativity. Crazy T had described The Flow as a joining of sense and consciousness. He never mentioned how dark this ghoulish consciousness could be.

I sensed The Flow was a portal, the ultimate force that would drive some teens to heaven and others to hell. But it was dormant at the moment, collecting energy. It would take a huge event to trigger it, to darken enough souls to open the portal to hell. But it was close, and the Takers waiting inside only fueled its negative energy.

"You might as well give up right now," one voice said. "Once you taste of The Flow, you never leave."

"Once a Taker, always a Taker," another told me.

I saw the memories I'd rather forget as I bled my pain into The Flow. There I was, partying away at the age of thirteen, already on my way to alcoholism. I was amazed; I thought I looked so sexy, so fun, so alive. Instead, I was a kid in a t-shirt pouring beer over myself in an effort to appear to be something, someone I was not. To see my tiny, dimpled cheeks, my kid body, still developing, made me sick. If I were to see that same body in a school photo, I'd guess that I was eight, maybe nine, years old. Instead, I was thirteen, and this was the path I'd chosen. The overwhelming drain of wasted life cascaded into The Flow, and I felt weaker, more jaded.

"I wasted my life," I said.

"Life is a waste," another voice told me.

"It would've been better for your mother if you were never born at all."

One voice, one Taker, fed off of another, until the negativity was so deep it wrapped itself like a straightjacket around me.

"You were sure ugly," a voice said.

"Look at you—you were such a loser," another told me. "And you think those people really liked you for you? You really think they were your friends?"

"You have no friends," yet another voice said.

I felt crowded by the dark energy until I saw that the energy manifested itself in different places. There was a party in Burgundy Hill, and the Takers cruised the bodies of the living, looking for any who might be killed that night. I was in the belly of an insatiable force, a dark monster full of voices, all calling out for drink, drugs, or one more day of life to be squandered. Some cried out about how unfair it was that they were there at all, while other voices called them stupid, ugly, or worthless, just like the voices that spoke to me.

There was this one kid at the party, clearly drunk to the point of passing out. He lay in a heap, laughing, then belching, then lying there, his face contorted, like he was suffering from alcohol poisoning. I tried to help, but I was pushed further back into The Flow. The darker Taker energies manifested themselves, one in the form of a lanky pitch black ghost with no eyes and the edge of a smashed bottle in one hand. I sensed this was a boy, once, who died in an alcohol-induced rage, and the Takers in The Flow were pushing him to egg on the boy, to get him up, to get him violent. Some other drunk kid stumbled over the boy, and the two argued. I saw the boy take a bottle, smash the end of it, just as the Taker urged him to do. He struck the other boy across the cheek until friends came and broke it up. The energy of The Flow grew, then waned as the situation deteriorated.

Immediately, the Takers whipped throughout the party. The Flow, a dark mist of disembodied energy, divided, in small black waves, until they found the next likely candidate, a kid fighting to get a car to start.

The kid giggled as the car shorted out, then swore. It was obvious from the slurring that this kid was also drunk. The Takers used their manipulation of energy to jumpstart the car just so this drunk could take death to the streets. I felt another Taker, a girl with half her head missing, step forward, propelling this drunk to make the same mistakes she made, to end up just the way she did. The kid did crash into a pole, but was rendered unconscious. A few Takers still swarmed around him, to see whether he might be taken for dead.

I attempted to call out, to warn the boy, but The Flow turned on me. All I could say was, "People do care."

"Did they care about you?" a Taker asked.

"Your classmates will be better off dead," another Taker added.

"They will be—shortly," yet another Taker taunted.

The Takers laughed. Even their laughter sounded painful.

The Flow showed me a picture of the school in the days after my death. My friends still struggled, but the faculty spoke of being anxious to put the episode, as they called my death, behind them. They complained about how the kids were unfocused, about how the lazier ones used it as an excuse to do no schoolwork. Even a few of the kids walking by said, "It's not like she really did anything important. People should just move on."

Oddly, I didn't feel insulted.

"I hope they do move on," I said.

The Flow began convulsing, shaking me free.

Yet, the Takers held on.

"They have nothing to move on from," one Taker said.

"You were a drunk," another Taker added.

"You were such a waste," multiple Taker voices insisted.

I was shown countless images of myself wasted, too drunk to even walk. I saw myself coming home after school, grabbing the whiskey in the top cabinet, reserved for my mother's hard work days, and having a few drinks. I saw the occasional drink grow and grow until I knew where all the places to get illegal liquor were, until I memorized my mother's credit card to order bottles over the Internet. I knew I'd always be home first, that she'd be working, and I found easy ways to support my habit until I had as great a party reputation as any girl at my school.

I fought against the images, fighting to project visions of myself loving, caring for someone else, fighting nights to stay sober, if only to lose again. I showed moments when I reached out to friends, moments when I was human.

Slowly, I began to hear less of The Flow. It still held me; I'd never truly break free. No Taker ever does. But I knew I had my own will, that I didn't just have to go along with the other Takers if I kept something of my goodness, something of my humanity.

I'd be a reject from hell, never dark enough for the Takers to drive me there.

Just yet.

And as I woke up from Crazy T's curse, I sensed that The Flow worked two ways. He could sense me, but I could also sense his thoughts. He knew my fears, but I also knew his.

I realized then that the woman's name was Lisa Walters and that she was Crazy T's obsession once upon a time. I knew that her rejection of him fueled his rage, that the loss of her, the humiliation he faced, the shame of his father, that they all made him angry enough to kill.

And I knew just where to find her when the time came.

In fact, I still owed her a detention.

ONE DAY TO GO

CHAPTER 8

Throughout school the next day, all the kids could talk about was the Friday game against Franklin Shore. Alex and the other players were on the news, dedicating the game to my memory. If I didn't stop Zipper, I wondered if they would play back that clip after the bleachers and the better part of town was blown away.

Takers swarmed the school, walking behind nearly any kid they could get next to. They whispered lies, encouraged the players to talk up the game. They hardly needed to. Not even a few small town deaths could stop Burgundy Hill from competing for the state championship. As if Alex, Tom, and the rest of the players weren't arrogant enough, they actually allowed local TV cameras on site to talk to the students about their memory of me and the dedication of the game.

"She was a sister to me," Gretchen said, breaking down.

We barely talked.

Alex, the photogenic captain of the team, said only: "She will be missed."

I was the love of his early life, but he said only four words.

The Takers laughed at that one, held at bay only by the sheer volume of explosives already lying in wait.

Tom, looking especially arrogant, said before the cameras: "We'll play like never before. I plan to make my first two goals for Fay and Kyla."

The principal escorted the TV crew to a few classes where crisis counselors were still at work with small groups of teens.

"What's your favorite memory of Fay and Kyla?" the counselor asked the kids.

It was a phony question, purely for the cameras.

"She helped me learn how to ride a bike," one girl said.

It was Sue, my old drinking buddy. I'm sure she was right. I did help her ride without training wheels because I was the big girl who beat her out of the gate. But I couldn't help but notice that she didn't mention getting drunk with me on weekends or even at school. I couldn't count the amount of times we snuck into the bathroom to drink at our leisure. Then there were the times, too many to count, when we took out water bottles in class and took a swig of whatever kept us buzzed that day. The teachers looked right at us as we did it, and they often just continued with their lessons. I'd even gotten drunk in Mrs. Walters' class, and she was a good teacher.

As for Sue, she'd have some scotch before she left school that day.

"That's good," the crisis counselor said. "Why don't we explore those memories more?"

The reporter cut from the scene to pitch the game as a great memorial to the traditions of Burgundy Hill High in the face of overwhelming tragedy.

At an angle, watching the reporters with red, squinty eyes, was Steph. She shook her head and walked off. I followed her.

From her aura alone, I could tell that Steph had some restless nights. Her dreams, mired in Takers, were full of dark shadows and voices that sounded like her mother. Deep black chasms opened up and even familiar town streets were cast in endless shadow. She hadn't slept a full night since the crash and though she was cleared from the hospital without serious injuries, she was still hurting from some bruises and what could quite possibly turn out to be an undiagnosed concussion.

I appeared next to her as she brushed her teeth and went through the nightly ritual of going to bed. The girl was still in shock. Her whole life had been crushed and mired worse than the body of the caravan. In her aura floated moments of emotional memory, and I could see her with her mother. They had a special relationship, the kind I never really had with my own mother. They drove everywhere together, shopped for Coach purses together, laughed at the same inside jokes, and even called the same guys cute. Lynn, Steph's mom, was the version of herself Steph wanted to be, and in one night's drinking I took her away forever.

Steph finished washing her face and headed towards her bedroom.

She'd have to cross her mother's room diagonally to get to hers. She'd have to hear her father crying in there alone. Steph was close to her dad, too, but it wasn't the same. She peeked towards the doorway, but she ultimately crept into bed. How wounded her energy was, full of fading blues and whites. She was a void, still too frozen and shaken by the events to have a good cry. As she got in the covers, she looked over to a picture of her mother and her out in front of some lake, on matching water skis. She wasn't much of a tomboy, and the skis weren't exactly a natural fit, but the smile shared between mother and daughter was real, too real for my comfort.

Steph got between the covers and just lied there. Judging from the aura, she was thinking about her mother, about her crying father, about her own inability to cry. Her frustration and shock easily grew into anger. I sensed that she was angry enough to strike a girl and that she'd been using a few drinks here and there to take the edge off. She felt especially guilty, given that my drinking took the life of her mother, but she couldn't talk to her father and she found herself short on friends. No one could take the place of her mother, and now pictures like the one on her bureau were all that she had left. She was spiraling already. Takers fed off of her blue and red swirling energy and pushed her on with darker thoughts of her friends, of me, of the pain she'd always feel if she chose to go ahead and face reality. Every time her wounds smarted enough for her to cry, Takers ate away at the emotion, pigging out on it, fueling the anger that fed them even more. If Steph survived the shooting, which was unlikely, I could tell that in a year or two she'd take my place. She'd give in to a life of drugs, alcohol, cutting, and promiscuity, just to channel all that emotion, to keep sane. I had to do something.

"Can you hear me?" I whispered to her.

No response.

"I never got to apologize," I said.

Steph rolled over, too lost in her own thoughts to hear mine.

"You have so much to live for," I told her.

As she drifted off into a fitful, crying sleep, I showed her images of herself and of a man she might marry, if she chose a different path. I showed her an image of my ex-boyfriend. There were images of a wedding, with white crystal vases and silky floral arrangements, of her mother, standing there, watching the new bride receive her fist kiss, crying.

Steph half awoke, wondering if what she saw was real. The red of her aura grew. The feeling was too raw.

My mother will never see my wedding, she thought to herself.

I tried to spread images of light, but I was still a creature of darkness. The Taker in me fed on her despair.

Out of the corner of the window, I saw Crazy T smiling, looking in.

"Don't worry," he said to me. "In two days, her grief will be at an end. You can finish pigging out on her energy then."

Steph lied there, stifling her cries. I sat on the bed next to her, trying to show her images of who and what I was, of the plan she'd have to play a part in. I failed. She kept sobbing as quietly as she could, hoping her father wouldn't hear her. I never felt so alone as when I saw her there, crying because of me.

The strength of their energy brought me to Mandy's mom who was by Mandy's side, in the hospital.

Mandy had awoken, but was unable to move her lower body.

Despite the meeting of our spirits, she was scared, deathly afraid, as she awoke. She felt that her lower legs should move, but there was nothing there, no motion, no sign of life in her lower body. She was crying out, and her mom was looking for a nurse. Mrs. Bilki, Mandy's mom, pressed the emergency call button, but the hospital was full of overworked nurses who had to attend to too many rooms. Hers wasn't the only emergency of the hour.

When a nurse finally came, Mrs. Bilki called out, "My daughter. She's screaming."

"I'll get the doctor," the nurse said.

She walked out, leaving Mrs. Bilki to take her daughter's hand.

"I can't move," Mandy hollered.

"It's your spine," her mom told her. "It was damaged in the accident."

Mandy stopped hollering. The thought struck her.

"I'm never going to walk again, am I?" she asked.

"I don't know," her mother said.

By the time the doctor got there, Mandy was bawling. There was anger in her aura, a pale red, and a chalky gray, the sign of her immense gloom.

The doctor came and said, "Hello, Mandy. I'm Dr. Nordstom. I want to tell you first how lucky you are to have survived. If your spine or neck took any other blow, you may not have been so lucky."

"Lucky?" she asked. "You call this lucky?"

Dr. Nordstom said nothing.

"Is this my life?" Mandy asked bitterly.

"It'll take time," Dr. Nordstom said. "But we have specialists looking at your case this very moment and facilities that can help you train your body to move to the fullest extent possible. You do have the use of your arms. That will help."

"Help me to do what?"

"Get around."

Mandy thought of me briefly; I could swear she looked right at me.

I'll be here, I whispered.

I knew even that might prove an empty lie.

Mrs. Bilki was there when Mandy's father came in with the first hospital bill. He didn't show it to Mandy's mom, who was too busy holding Mandy's hand. I could see it, though. It was already high enough to be a second mortgage.

Mr. Bilki had just gotten off the phone for the first of many times with the insurance company.

He'd just learned that on top of dealing with a grieving daughter, on top of a major life adjustment, he'd soon be in for the fight of his life: the fight with his insurer.

He blamed me, and he blamed my mother for all of this. His aura was a vermillion fire.

Just as soon as he got off the phone with his insurer, he called a friend of his, a lawyer.

CHAPTER 9

Keepers swarmed around my mother as she met with the women from the Burgundy Hill Mothers against Drinking and Driving.

The Burgundy Hill Mothers hadn't let up on calls, or on emails, since my mother first called them back. Though she was conflicted about joining, my mother agreed to meet, to accept some kind of condolence basket that, for some reason, they thought was in good taste.

I knew my mom. She was always a private woman, kind of the opposite of me. She stopped taking phone calls from well-wishers, and she stopped opening her email after the funeral. She just wanted time to adjust, to find a new normal. But it was far too soon. She'd clean up after messes that weren't there, find the time to paint the bathroom now that she wasn't dealing with phone calls from guidance counselors and endless parent-teacher meetings. She kept the pictures of me all around, as if I were just on some long trip. She couldn't bear to take them down. If only she could speak to Steph, if only Steph could speak to her, they might find some comfort. But their only connection was an accident both wanted to forget.

"I really do appreciate the support," Mom said.

She took a basket from the Burgundy Hill Mothers and placed it next to the dozens of others on the table.

"We know what you're feeling," one mother, a woman named Beth, said. "I went through the same thing with my Eric. I can't tell you how many times I still think of him."

"I'll bet," Mom said.

Her aura was a pink fading to gray, the sign of her distress.

"We meet once a month," another mother, Yvonne, said. "We organize awareness events, speak at schools, help organize local safe proms."

But that won't bring my daughter back.

The thought was strong, written all over my mother's aura in blues and grays.

"Our goal is to make Burgundy Hill a safe community," Yvonne added, as if drinking could be stamped out anywhere.

A little late for Fay, Mom thought.

The auras of the women mingled into a majestic silver. There was nothing sadder in spirit than a grieving mother. Keepers did their best to console them whenever possible.

"I'm not ready," Mom said, simply.

"We just want you to know you're not alone," Beth told my mother, giving her a hug.

Mom felt like breaking down, but the situation was too uncomfortable. She'd never cry in front of strangers; her pride was too great.

"I know," Mom said instead.

She didn't know.

"I see you're redecorating the place," Yvonne said to her.

Mom had tried to hide the fresh paint, but the smell was too great.

"Just something I've been meaning to get around to," she said.

Yvonne nodded. Her eyes showed that she understood, that maybe she had done the same thing when her time had come.

"We'll stay in touch," she said.

Yvonne and Beth hugged Mom, and just as quickly as they were there, they were through the door and my mother was by herself.

The Keepers gave her energy, helping her avoid completely breaking down.

I went up and kissed her. I swear she almost sensed my presence.

But then she was back in the bathroom, adding an unnecessary coat of honey-colored paint.

I stayed with my mother the rest of the night, hoping, praying that she'd finally sleep. She cried until two-thirty when her exhaustion took over. She'd be up again at five, hide as much of her weariness as she could with eyeliner, and then be on her way to the law office. The lawyer wouldn't even ask about how she was doing, just about some papers she had to file that would grant an extension on a trial date. It was official: Mandy's parents were suing. Because of my drunk driving, my mother could lose everything she ever owned.

Even more awkwardly, my father was there.

I hadn't seen him since he walked out on our family years ago, but Mom's lawyer dug him up. He looked older, with curled black and gray hair, a deep sagging chin and bags under his black eyes. He looked fatter too, especially for a guy who worked with his hands. His aura was a beaten gray. I could tell he'd rather be anywhere else, but he was still my legal guardian.

"Hello, Helen," he said.

My mother nodded.

"I'd been meaning to talk to you."

"Is that so?"

My mother tried not to put too much vinegar into her words, but the weight of my death, of my painful upbringing, was too great.

"I'd been thinking that we could revisit child support," he said. "Now this."

"You missed her whole life," Mom said.

My father paused. "I'm paying for that," he said. "I don't need you to remind me."

"The only time you ever paid for anything was when a court order took it out of your cheque," Mom told him.

"I paid for the fun—"

My biological father stopped short. Both he and Mom looked towards the ground.

Seeing them standing there, surrounded by their auras, it was clear. Their auras clashed so much, giant swirls of red and gray, that I had no doubt that these people should have never produced a child.

"Mr. and Ms. DeSoto," the lawyer said. "Let's step inside."

Step inside they did.

The lawyer, a man named Kirk Simmons, pored through the police and insurance records, piecing together the tale of my fateful night.

"I'm sorry," he said, "but we're going to have to get the story precise before I decide whether I can take you on."

After the lawyer rather graphically described my passing, he asked: "Were either of you there?"

"No," Mom answered. "I was awoken by the police and called in to verify that the body was..."

My father just shook his head.

"Did you know about your daughter's alcohol problem?" Mr. Simmons continued.

"My daughter was not an alcoholic," my father said, a little too loudly. Mom just kept looking down.

"She was," Mom said.

"You knew?" my father asked.

"It's not like you were there to tell," she said to him. "I knew. I'd see the bottles, hear her stumbling in drunk late at night." Mom looked so old as she gathered her thoughts, pulled from the blue of her aura. "I couldn't admit it, though," she said. "She was my girl."

"No one is saying this is your fault, Ms. DeSoto," Mr. Simmons said.

"Mandy's mother is," Mom replied. "And maybe she's right." There was a pause, and then Mom added: "But I can't afford to give her anything."

"How much does she want?" my father asked.

That was the one question that swirled in his aura, the one thing he really cared about.

"She wants nearly two million dollars," Mr. Simmons answered, "the estimated cost of caring for her daughter throughout her life minus what your insurance from the accident will cover, provided your insurer actually covers the full amount, which is rare."

"That's robbery," my father said. "She wants to get rich, plain and simple."

"In all likelihood, her daughter will never walk again," Mr. Simmons said. "The amount may seem astronomical, but it's not, compared to other costs I've seen in trials involving paralysis. If anything, it's modest."

"But it's not our fault," this man, my father, said.

"Fay was a minor and her primary caretaker knew that she had an alcohol problem, yet failed to get her treatment for her disease," the lawyer said. "Her secondary caretaker wasn't even visiting her regularly. That can make the parents culpable in the eyes of a judge."

"Can you get us out of this?" my father asked.

"I'm sorry," Mr. Simmons said. "Given what you've said here, which wasn't in the original email, I'm not so sure. Frankly, I don't think it's in your best interest that I handle this case. But I can refer you to a colleague. He's handled such cases before."

"How much will he cost?" my father asked.

"He'll talk numbers with you," Mr. Simmons said.

He handed Mom the name of another, much cheaper, lawyer, and then shook her hand. Mr. Simmons quickly shook my father's hand and then guided my parents to the door.

"What were you thinking?" my father asked in the parking lot. "Why didn't you say you didn't even know she was drinking?"

"Because I did. I just looked away," Mom said.

"Now we're screwed."

"I'm sure you'll find a way out of paying," Mom said.

My father shook his head, walked towards the car. "You calling the new lawyer?" he asked.

"We can't afford a lawyer," Mom said, "unless you can pay for one. I'll ask the court to appoint one."

With that, my father drove off, and Mom was left putting the lawyer card in her purse, standing, as she always did, all alone.

⁓⁓⁓

I never thought of Mrs. Walters as beautiful until I saw her aura, this gentle mist of gold, white, and purple. She was a dignified woman who always found a teachable moment. Once, when I was depressed over

Alex, she told me of how she first met her husband in college. It was a small gesture, but one filled with hope, and it meant a lot to me that October morning long before I knew I'd soon be dead. She stood only five feet without heels on, and she had honey-colored hair in a bun that looked a tad retro. She had pale white cheeks with tiny brown freckles, which I thought looked funny in an adult, but underscored her natural beauty. The boys loved her, but she was a mom to the end, and the way she spoke to them reminded them too much of Mother for the gossip over her looks to spread too far.

I never thought she was young enough to be in high school with Crazy T. I never thought that his entire death began and ended around her. She was the girlfriend of one jock Crazy T shot down. It was over Crazy T looking at her longingly in class one day that they invited him to the party in the woods by the school, where they humiliated him. She was the Helen of Burgundy Hill High, the face that launched a thousand fights.

Here she was, years later, passing out the next English assignment I'd never do, not that I did many when I was alive. It was a poem the kids had to write describing how they felt about what happened to me, Kyla, and Steph. I thought it was a rather edgy assignment, and some kids looked up at her with pleading eyes and asked, "Can we do something else?"

I wasn't offended. I understood that when deaths happen in a small town, it's death overkill. Everyone cries; everyone's affected. There's a beauty to that. But it can be too much for some students who think stressing over sex and the prom is more than enough at the moment.

"I'll let you choose the topic," Mrs. Walters said to the students, "on two conditions. It has to mean something to you. And you have to give the poem to someone."

"What?" Sue asked.

"Write the poem for someone," Mrs. Walters said. "A poem without an audience is like music without sound. Does it exist in the first place?"

The class murmured.

"Are you going to write a poem?" Alex asked her.

She looked at him blankly.

"Would you like me to?" she asked.

"Yeah," the class said unanimously.

It was a good save, but I saw the look in Alex's eyes, a look I once put there, a look of pain.

He wasn't going to let go that easily.

"I mean, you lost some people in high school too, didn't you?" he asked.

I couldn't say how Alex knew about it. There were rumors, I suppose, but it was one question we just knew not to ask. No one ever talked about the shooting as the years rolled on. No one wanted to admit that the halls we'd grown so secure in could become a maze of bullet fire.

"I lost three classmates," Mrs. Walters said. "One was my boyfriend."

Mrs. Walters teared up. A few of the kids did too, including Alex, who did his best to hide it.

"Why are you still here?" Alex asked.

"She's the teacher," Sue said. "Where else should she be?"

"No, I mean why teach here—after what happened?" Alex asked.

Mrs. Walters looked past the students, into a darker past all her own.

"It's complicated," she said. "Maybe I'll tell you my story in a poem if you tell me yours in one."

The class looked at Alex. He usually stopped doing his classwork once the soccer season wound down.

"I suck at poetry," he said. "Poetry sucks. Why write it at all?"

"Poetry only sucks if you force yourself to write the poem," she said. "You have to let the poem write itself through you. You have to start with what you feel."

"I don't know what I feel."

"That's why we need poetry."

There were a few more murmurs. Apparently, Burgundy High kids didn't agree that poetry was necessary at all.

"Okay. We have some time left. Why don't you start drafting?" Mrs. Walters asked the class. "Channel your feelings."

"Do we have to?" Sue asked.

Mrs. Walters just shook her head. The class took out their pens and got started.

I watched as Alex began work on his poem.

It was a kiddy poem, the kind I might've written, but profound for Alex. To me, poems always had to have rhyme, like it gave order to life or something.

Summer Kiss

That day by the boathouse shore
when the sun was high
we heard the ocean tides roar
and kissed the first kiss goodbye.
We knew summer was through
and so were we
too old for first love true
too young for eternity.
Love can last forever;

it's too bad relationships die so quickly.
If we were the way I felt when we were together
~~You'd never have cheated on me.~~
We'd have been a couple for eternity.

Granted, Alex screwed up the rhyme scheme a bit, but who was I to judge? I was moved. I was amazed at the emotion that just came gushing out of him. I leaned over to kiss him and felt the warmth of the Keepers surrounding Mrs. Walters.

"Don't read it," Alex said as Mrs. Walters came closer.

"You can share it when you're ready."

"When will you share your poem, then?"

"I'll write it tonight," she said, "and share it tomorrow."

Mrs. Walters looked at the clock, announced that the period was a minute away from ending.

In the far corner of the class, surrounded by Takers, was Zipper. He was so quiet, so normal, I'd barely noticed him. I might not have noticed if it hadn't been for a few Takers swirling by his aura.

He started a poem, too. He tore it up.

As he did, I saw:

Life will be over by week's end.
It died the day she did.
The world's ending.
The torment will cease;
None will remain alive.
Just one thing to consider:
Would I have lived if the world was worth living for?

The bell rang, and a shred of the poem made it to the floor. The class bolted out the door. Mrs. Walters walked the aisles between desks to clean up for the next class. She found only a line of the poem: "Would I have lived if the world was worth living for?" She put it on her desk. From the swirling energies of her aura, I could tell that she was curious about the author. She'd be too late if she waited to find out. But the next class was coming in, already complaining about the assignment. Mrs. Walters forgot about the line of poetry and fell back into teacher mode.

Later that day, the school psychologist started meeting kids in small groups.

Alex and Zipper happened to be in the same group, the ex-boyfriend group. Alex couldn't believe it, but technically Mrs. Cowell was right. Zipper was my first kiss, my first boyfriend. Alex was my last.

"We just want you to have a place to talk," Mrs. Cowell said, "to share your feelings and memories of Fay and Kyla."

Alex just shook his head.

The gesture, ever so small, caught Mrs. Cowell's eye.

"Alex?" she asked.

"Why can't you just leave it alone?" he asked. "All week we hear you going on and on about how it's okay to cry, about how everything will work itself out. It won't. Fay's dead. They couldn't even show her body at her funeral. That's not all right."

"No, it's not," Mrs. Cowell agreed. "I know if I had a girlfriend—"

"You don't know," Alex said. "And she was my *ex*-girlfriend."

"Ex-girlfriend."

Alex clammed up. Zipper just sat there, looking at him. Their auras were so red hot I could barely tell where one ended and the other began.

"Does anyone else feel that way?" Mrs. Cowell asked.

No one else spoke up. A few of the guys, like Tom, were interesting selections. Just a few months ago, Tom and Alex were at each other's throats over me, until Alex moved on, decided I wasn't worth it. Tom decided the same.

"Does anyone want to talk about Fay or Kyla?" Mrs. Cowell asked.

All eyes shot downward. Mrs. Cowell fished around the room for any wayward glance. She thought she found one in Zipper.

"John?" she asked.

"Zipper," he said.

Alex murmured. The gesture was not lost on Zipper.

"I didn't know her," Zipper said.

In that comment, I felt his sadness. I felt his longing for us to be closer and his pain that we'd never be, not in life.

Mrs. Cowell caught the intonation, too.

"Did you want to?" she asked Zipper.

Alex studied the expression on Zipper's face. For a moment, Zipper's face trembled with what could almost be called emotion.

"I want this erased," Zipper said. "I want everything erased."

"Everything? That's cold," Alex said.

"Cold is allowing your girlfriend to get drunk and then drive," Zipper said.

Alex stood up, standing over Zipper. "Are you deaf?!" he yelled. "She wasn't my girlfriend then! Besides, what do you know about girlfriends, anyway?"

Zipper smiled eerily at the provoked figure. Both auras were rippling with red and black energy.

"Alex," Mrs. Cowell said. Her soothing pink aura spread over theirs as she said: "John is just—"

"Zipper."

"Zipper is just speaking his mind."

"If he speaks any more of it, I'll..." Alex began muttering.

"You'll what?" Zipper asked. "I don't drive drunk...unlike you."

Alex turned and went through the door.

Watching Alex storm through the school hallways and out, so that no one would see him cry, was painful. His aura became like blood flowing, wounded as he was. Zipper's words had hit him hard, mainly because they were words he'd said to himself. To know that others, outsiders, viewed it the same way simply served as confirmation. He punched a wall and then wandered out a door.

Zipper, still seated, was quiet as a few other kids went on about me. Inside, he was the way Alex was on the outside: angry, incredibly so. His aura was all over the place, surrounded by mocking Takers, and I knew it'd take just one or two more eruptions like this to get him to pull the trigger.

That night, Mrs. Walters shed off the years that stood between her and her high school experience.

She sat at an oak table with her husband, a financier, and talked openly of her day.

"The students are really having a hard time of it," she told her husband.

"Are all three girls dead?" her husband asked.

He didn't wait for an answer, but dug his knife into the steak his wife had prepared.

"Mandy's still holding on," she said. "I had the kids write poems. I might mail a few out to her."

Her husband looked up. His brown eyes held hers. "Are you sure that's wise?" he asked.

"Why wouldn't it be?"

"It's so close to the event. Do the kids really need to be writing about it?"

"What else is poetry for?"

Mrs. Walters took a sip of red wine, swished it around her mouth, swallowed, and looked at her husband. She was circling around the topic that was truly on her mind.

"I remember how much writing helped me when Steve got shot," she said.

Her husband looked down, concentrating on the steak, which was a bit red for his liking.

"I can throw it back on the grill," Mrs. Walters said.

"No need," her husband replied.

"I wrote and wrote when Steve died," Mrs. Walters continued. "I can still remember that day like it was yesterday."

She could too. I could see her high school self standing in front of a mirror, deciding what to wear. Her biggest challenge of the day was a black blouse Steve liked and a sheik vermillion skirt she adored. The skirt won. It would prove an especially ironic choice of color.

She was in the cafeteria for study hall when the first shots rang out. She didn't hear them, too busy gossiping with her friends about how far she and Steve went the other night. The moment a slightly less portly Mr. Higgins came stumbling in, his science lecture notes in his hands, she could tell that something was wrong. His face was red and scrunched up, yet he was sweating as he whispered something to the study proctor. The school was going into lockdown. They wanted nothing said to the students to avoid panic. But it was too late. From the far rear window of the cafeteria, Mrs. Walters, then just Lisa, saw kids running, spattered with their own blood and the blood of others. She stood there a moment, too shocked to say anything. More observant kids filmed the entire episode on their cells and were texting pictures back and forth. Within a minute, the story was around the school and kids knew that something was up, that an explosion had happened by the gym and that people were hurt. It wasn't until the photos of the kids running towards the cafeteria hallway surfaced that it became clear: Students had been shot.

"That psycho," Paul, a buff jock and acquaintance of Lisa, called out.

Blood stained his legs as he searched up and down to see how bad the wounds were. Parts of kids had fallen on him, but he wasn't hurt.

"What's going on?" Becky, a friend of Lisa's, asked.

"Matt and a few other kids got him," the kid said. "Not before he fired, though."

"Who fired?"

Paul looked right at Lisa, his eyes full of hidden light.

"Teddy Berschmire," he said.

"Crazy T?" Lisa asked.

"He shot..."

Paul couldn't say it. Lisa just looked at him and started bawling.

"Is he still alive?" she managed to ask.

Paul looked down and lost his eyes to the floor.

"I'm sorry," he said.

This one moment, born of a demented brain, would come to define the rest of Mrs. Walters' life. Crazy T may have been obsessed with her, but she launched an obsession of her own: to help kids in need so that they would never turn out like Crazy T did.

How to capture all of that in a poem?

All these years later, she sat eating steak with her husband, still alive, randomly so.

"It must have been awful," Mr. Walters said in response to his wife's earlier question. "Could you pass the A-1 sauce?"

Mrs. Walters shook her head and reached for the sauce. Her hand still shook, all these years later, as she handed her husband the condiment. Mr. Walters saw but just continued cutting into his steak. He'd heard the story before. It never ended well.

That night, Zipper was given special orders: to make sure the fields were clean for the championship game. It was an exhausting process, cleaning up anything from wrappers tossed carelessly by kids skipping out on gym class to mowing and making sure the field lines were freshly painted. But Zipper had a natural talent for making everything look just perfect.

Zipper sat on the mower, ear buds in, zigzagging along the edge of the pavement, in a circuitous route he had memorized after months of planting explosives.

He hit a snag. There was an explosion—a small one, but one that could've blown the whole school away.

Zipper tore out his ear buds and looked around. His boss, Mr. Peterson, a fat, bald, stocky man who still bore some signs of his former athleticism, rushed to the scene, beer can still in hand.

"What the hell?" Mr. Peterson asked.

Zipper shrugged his shoulders.

"This piece of crap needs to get looked at," Zipper said, pointing down at the mower.

"I've never heard the thing make that noise in seven years," Mr. Peterson said. "You must not be handling it right."

Mr. Peterson went over to the mower, started examining the mower as it ran.

A pipe choked out some smoke, sounded a bit gruff.

"That wasn't the sound I heard," Mr. Peterson said.

"Yeah—it was worse before," Zipper told him.

"Let me know if it happens again," Mr. Peterson replied.

"Don't you want me to stop mowing?" Zipper asked.

"Not on your life," Mr. Peterson said. "Get these fields ready."

Zipper smiled, nodded, and put his ear buds back in. He started mowing again, leaving Mr. Peterson to his beer and a cloud of dust.

THE DAY OF THE SHOOTING:

Morning

CHAPTER 10

Steph and her friends walked in with the T-shirts she had specially made. On the back, a picture of her mom holding her. On the front, the words, in bright blood red: "Forget Fay."

In her first position class, the students were already buzzing.

Mr. Higgins knew something big was going on, as he managed to get two phones from the kids in the first ten minutes of class. Teens were never that sloppy with their phones. Something was up.

Then Steph walked in, not even flinching as she headed to her seat.

A group of kids murmured, looking from their old Bunsen burners to the shirt.

"Steph," Mr. Higgins said. "Come here."

Steph marched up to Mr. Higgins's desk, making no effort at concealment.

"We're all happy you're back," Mr. Higgins said. "None of us know what you're going through. But that shirt—"

"I have the *right* to wear this shirt," Steph said.

Her voice didn't quiver in the slightest. She'd clearly rehearsed the conversation many times in her head.

"Even if you do—" Mr. Higgins said.

"I do," Steph insisted.

"Does having a right make it right?" Mr. Higgins inquired.

"Did Fay have the right to kill my mom?" Steph asked in reply.

Mr. Higgins took a breath and examined the angry young girl before him. The class was deathly silent, listening, pretending to fool with the burners.

"Fay," Mr. Higgins pleaded.

"I'm not taking off this shirt."

Steph stood there, inflexible.

"Why don't you go talk to Mrs. Cowell?" Mr. Higgins suggested. "You'll feel better."

"I'm not going anywhere," Steph said. "And talking isn't going to make anything better."

Her aura was so full of vibrant reds, so wounded, so angry.

"The back of the shirt is so beautiful," Mr. Higgins said. "Your mother would be so proud. Why—"

"Don't speak of my mother!"

"Please, Steph," Mr. Higgins pleaded. "That shirt's hurting some of Fay's friends."

"Good. Those alcoholics deserve it."

"Steph, please change shirts."

"No."

"I can't have you wearing that shirt in this class," Mr. Higgins said. "It's hurting your friends."

"To hell with them. They weren't even at the funeral. They're not my friends," Steph said.

Mr. Higgins picked up the phone and dialed down to Mrs. Cowell. His only words: "Please come immediately."

I sensed from his aura that this was the only time in thirty years he'd ever uttered those words.

"Really?" Steph challenged. "You're going to force me out over this?"

"No one's forcing you out," Mr. Higgins said.

Mrs. Cowell heard and said she'd be on her way. Mr. Higgins hung up the phone.

"If you force me to leave, if you force me to take off this shirt, I will sue," Steph said. "You're obstructing my education, Mr. Higgins, and that I can't have."

Steph wore a bitter smirk on her face as she spoke the words.

Mr. Higgins scratched his beard, as if that was somehow the appropriate response. Words failed him.

Steph stared deeply into him before turning to the class.

"She killed my mother," she said to the students. "I won't let you pretend she was some kind of saint. She was a selfish, thoughtless, nasty drunk, and I'm paying the price for it. So are her mother and her boyfriend, and so is everyone else who hung out with her."

The kids turned from their thirty-year-old Bunsen burners, certain that this experiment was much more interesting than the one they were conducting. No one said a word, though. Their auras were all over the place, retreating as much as possible from the flaming red sun that was Steph's aura.

"No one's denying that you're paying a price you shouldn't have to," Mrs. Cowell said.

She had appeared in the doorway mid-speech, took to watching the exploding teenager before her eyes.

"I'm not leaving," Steph said. "You can't make me go. You can't ignore this!"

"No one's trying to ignore you, honey," Mrs. Cowell said.

"Up yours! What do you know?!" Steph asked. "Is it you going to bed every night crying?"

"No, it's not," Mrs. Cowell said.

"Then shut up," Steph said. "Don't tell me what to feel."

"I wouldn't dream of it," Mrs. Cowell said. "You have every right to feel how you're feeling."

"I don't need patronizing."

"I'm not patronizing. I'm agreeing," Mrs. Cowell said. "I don't know how you feel. Can you tell me?"

"What for?"

"To feel better."

"I can *never* feel better, not after this," Steph said. "Why can't you people just mind your own business?"

"You are our business," Mrs. Cowell said. "We care about you, Steph. We want to help."

"Well, you can't."

"Can you let us try?"

Steph took a step back, hardened her eyes.

"I know what you're trying to do. It won't work. This shirt isn't coming off," Steph said. "And I will *not* leave this room."

Steph sat down, staging a one-girl sit-in to make her point.

"Okay. Fair enough," Mrs. Cowell said.

Mrs. Cowell, old as she looked, came in and sat down right next to Steph.

"We'll talk here," Mrs. Cowell said.

"I don't want to talk," Steph said.

"Then we'll just sit," Mrs. Cowell said.

"Why?!" Steph asked.

Her voice sounded more like a whimper than an outcry.

"Because we want to be here for you," Mrs. Cowell said. "All of us."

Mr. Higgins' entire class, starting with Alex, came and sat down by Steph. Alex hugged Steph gently, like he might a sister. Steph pulled away, though her eyes had a reddish tinge from forcing back the tears. The other students sat around Steph, reaching out, grabbing a hand, patting a shoulder, calling out her name in encouragement. Finally, Mr. Higgins came. Far too big for the circle, he teetered, then sat in the doorway.

"Someone has to be the anchor," he said.

It was a stupid comment, out of place, without meaning, but the portly man trying to find room for a seat and barely fitting in the doorway gave the kids a laugh they sorely needed.

"I can't take off the shirt, not yet," Steph said after the laughter died down.

"Then keep it on," Mr. Higgins said. "Until you're ready."

Mr. Higgins knew he'd receive phone calls from parents over his words, but he didn't interfere. He just sat there. His entire class did, until Steph was able to get up, wipe the dirt off the back of her jeans, and walk out at the bell, as if nothing, and everything, had happened.

John Chatterly to the office, the intercom sounded out.

It was unusual to hear Zipper's real name, and I'd never once heard it over the intercom in all my years at Burgundy Hill High.

Zipper never heard his name called either.

He jolted in his seat near the end of Mrs. Walters' English class.

The class heard Mrs. Walters' poem after sharing one of their own. It was entitled "Lost Colors."

She had compared Steve and all of her friends to different colors from the rainbow. Corny, yes, but a more peaceful way of presenting what she had to say to already traumatized kids.

Zipper stood up in the middle of the poem, putting on his backpack right when Mrs. Walters said something like:

> *To lose a friend young*
> *is to lose a color*
> *Never before painted,*
> *A life never breaking from the clouds.*

Zipper stood there, looking at Mrs. Walters, and she looked back.

"I have to go," Zipper said.

"You won't need your backpack," Mrs. Walters told him.

"Five minutes left of class," Zipper said.

"Go ahead," Mrs. Walters replied.

She turned her attention back to her poem, back to the ghosts of twelve years ago.

Zipper began sweating heavily. He walked briskly, thinking back to last night, to his painting of the soccer lines, to the explosive that detonated, that could've ignited others and blown him up with the entire field. I read deeper into his aura. He wondered how he could be sure that everything was set, how he could be sure that the school kids would truly get blown away as his little legs carried him to the office door. He wondered what, exactly, the administration knew.

The moment Zipper stepped in the office, Mr. Buckley, the principal, stood waiting for him, a cop to his right.

Zipper's aura leapt. The Takers around him swirled in animosity. He did all he could not to go for his gun.

"John," Mr. Buckley said, calling him over.

Zipper stepped right up to the counter, still sweating.

"I have a message for you, John," Mr. Buckley said.

He handed Zipper a paper from Mr. Peterson.

"Need you out right at 2:30 to paint the fields again. Let Mr. Buckley know if you can stay."

"What happened?" John asked.

He kept his eyes on the cop.

"A few kids trespassed last night," Mr. Buckley said. "They damaged some of the lines. I sent Mr. Peterson to fix the fields, but he asked me to hand you a note."

Zipper breathed heavily, then calmed himself.

"I can stay," he said to Mr. Buckley.

"Thanks, John. I'll let Mr. Peterson know," Mr. Buckley said. "One more thing. Was anyone on the fields when you left?"

Zipper shook his head.

"Thanks," Mr. Buckley said. "You can go back to class now."

Zipper turned and left.

As Zipper walked down the hall, the quiet of class time was interrupted again.

Tom Harrington to the office, the intercom said.

Tom came right down, passing Zipper in the hall as he walked in.

Zipper smirked. Tom caught the smile.

"What?" he asked.

"Cop's waiting," Zipper told him. "Better walk in a straight line."

Tom fought to think of a putdown, but he was too nervous.

"They'll still let me play," was all he could think of to say.

He'd be right.

I still felt the party alive in the air.

The Taker in me could feel the loss of control.

I'd been blinded by Steph's rage, but the party was nearly as intense.

Not a week after my death, my friends threw a kegger right in the middle of the fields where they said they'd be champions in no time at all.

"For Fay," Tom screamed, standing on the top of his red Ford F-150 as he skidded around the fields.

I shook my head as Alex hung back, drinking just enough to be bitter.

Sue was there, swinging her hips, acting like the party girl I always strove to be. How stupid she looked, like some dumb, desperate girl who couldn't get a real guy interested any other way.

How sad, I thought, reliving the moments in Tom's aura as he stepped through the office door. *I'm not dead a week and already these drunks throw a party.*

The night was sacred to partiers; nothing ever interfered with the pre-game festivities.

"Just don't get behind the wheel," a drunken Tom joked.

"I bet you," Sue said, staggering closer. "I bet you I can drive drunk better than Fay. I can hold my liquor."

Tom signaled his friends; one, Bus, a big linebacker, threw her the keys.

"Prove it," Tom said.

"Tom," Alex called out drunkenly. "What the hell are you doing?"

"Winning some money. Fifty says you can't do it."

"Make it a hundred and you've got a bet," Sue said.

Tom nodded.

Sue got in, barely put her hands on the wheel as the tires screeched over the fresh field paint and she sped into the goal post.

Lights in the houses just opposite the fields went on. Tom called out a swear, pulled Sue from the wheel. She was giggling as the kids got in and Tom sped off.

I sensed all those thoughts in Tom's aura, yet, looking right at the cop, Officer Deriega, Tom said: "No. I know nothing of last night."

"Mr. Harold across the street said he saw you," Officer Deriega insisted. "He took down the plates."

"Well, he was wrong," Tom said.

"You were out last night, weren't you?" Officer Deriega asked.

"I know my rights; I want a lawyer," Tom said.

The principal smirked. "No one's accusing you of anything," he said. "We just want the truth."

"I let a friend borrow my car," Tom said. "I trusted her."

A few minutes later, the intercom called out again.

Sue Preston to the office.

I shook my head. I just knew she'd take the heat for her sometime lover.

"I have half a mind to cancel the game," Mr. Buckley said as he waited for Sue to arrive.

If only he did.

Judging from the text Tom sent Sue without even pulling the phone from his pocket, the game, and the shooting, were still on.

My mother sat by the phone, number in hand.

She hadn't spoken to Mandy's mom since the accident. Her lawyer advised her against it. But my mom was a lifelong friend of Mrs. Bilki and hated to let bad blood fester.

The phone rang and rang. I thought Mrs. Bilki recognized the number and wouldn't pick up. To my surprise, she did.

"Helen?" Mrs. Bilki asked.

There was a pause, a long one.

"It's me," Mom said. "I just wanted to call to say how sorry I am at the way everything's turned out."

"I have nothing to say to you," Mrs. Bilki said.

"Both our girls made a terrible decision that night," Mom said.

"But only one was behind the wheel," Mrs. Bilki told her.

"It could have been any of the girls."

"But it wasn't. And now Mandy may never walk again."

"But at least Mandy's alive," Mom said.

There was another pause.

"Is that why you've called? To tell me how lucky I am?"

"I called to say how sorry I was. I wished I had thought to get Fay treatment. I didn't."

"And now my Mandy will pay for it."

"Lacey, how long have we known each other?" Mom asked, using Mrs. Bilki's old nickname. "How long have we been friends? Let us work this out together."

"That's for the courts to decide," Mrs. Bilki said.

"But why?"

"I need to do what's best for my daughter," she said.

Mrs. Bilki breathed heavily as she turned over her next point.

"I know you did your best with Fay," she said. "I did my best with Mandy and look how it turned out. This is about accountability. Someone took my daughter's life away from her, and somebody needs to pay for that."

Mom started crying.

"Don't call again," Mrs. Bilki said. "Let the lawyers handle it."

Mrs. Bilki hung up. My mother was left eating the silence on the other end of the line.

The Takers swirled over the fields, keeping watch on the explosives so that no more went off until the hour was at hand.

Scenes of torn limbs, of rivulets of blood, filled the sky.

They were planning.

I wasn't quite one of them. I couldn't quite hear everything, but from what I gathered, they were positioning Zipper to be the one who kept watch on the fields during the game. This would give him access and make his targets that much easier to kill. He could get in enough shots to torment the parents who'd see their children slaughtered before their eyes. Then he'd trigger the explosives in a mass homicide and suicide that would be talked about for decades to come. Everyone would know the name of John Chatterly. Everyone would wear his blood.

The pain that surrounded the images overwhelmed me when I felt myself in the presence of a Keeper.

"Belinda, is that you?" I asked.

The light felt warmer, like a small taste of light. I knew that warmth; it was the openness of my grandparents' love. I only knew them when I was very young, but I could feel them there.

"What was that?" I asked.

"Heaven," Belinda said.

"Why show me now?" I asked.

"To give you strength," Belinda told me.

I could almost picture a crystal white shore with sparkling waters, an endless color-filled crest of trees and sands.

For me, the sands were empty.

"Save them while you still can," another Keeper voice said.

But I could see nothing more.

Takers swarmed around the images of flying limbs.

I could see only a wayward smile, sitting jaggedly on the ghostly pale face of Crazy T.

"All will die," he said.

"Over my dead body," I protested.

"That's already been arranged, now hasn't it?" he said.

He did have a point.

Last night, before the planned shooting, I tried to give Zipper one last innocent dream.

We were tiny kids then, all of us running along the Burgundy Sea Bike Path. We had just gotten out of school and still had a few old notebooks we threw into the sea. Zipper and I threw ours in at the same time as everyone else, turned, and smiled. Tom was there. Alex. Sue. Jessica. Kyla. We were friends once, long before words like *popularity* mattered.

There was simply cobalt water, smooth sand, and a golden light around everything.

"Quick," I said, tossing in my notebook. "If you hold on to the books long enough, school will suck you back in!"

Zipper and I laughed like the nine-year-olds we were as we tossed away the books.

He turned, caught my smile. Even at that young age, he liked me.

"They were your friends once," I said, stepping forward.

My black mists swirled around my silver radiance as I attempted to materialize in Zipper's head.

"Let them live," I said. "Let yourself live."

If I attempted to calm the sleeping Zipper, to soothe him, my dream only served to wake him up.

Zipper got out of his basement bed, took his picture of me, and went over to the drawer where he hid the guns he'd stolen from his father's gun cabinet.

I was at a loss until another Taker, Kyla, materialized before me.

Her smirk told me that she'd taken my peaceful vision, manipulated it. I shook my ghostly head, aware only too late that I'd played right into her hands.

At the end of that moment, the tossing of our books, Zipper stumbled, nearly fell into the ocean.

The other nine-year-olds laughed at him. I laughed at him. Zipper was many things, but a joke wasn't one of them. He respired so loudly he woke himself up, determined that I'd know just how tough he truly was.

He sat with his gun, much like a man might sit with a drink. He stroked the barrel, checked that it was loaded.

Kyla chided him on, showing him my laughing again and again, until it grew too loud for him to control.

I sought any warmth, any light, but her dark aura won over both of us.

She was so dark now, so without light, that I knew that this was the event that would bring her to hell.

Her power grew, but I planted one small image in Zipper's mind first.

"Can you believe John almost fell?" Kyla asked at the river's edge.

"John's cute," I said to Kyla as we walked away. "We don't need to lose the cute ones."

The thought calmed Zipper down for just a moment, brought him the vaguest hints of a smile. He then picked up the gun and made sure it was ready.

LATER ON THE DAY OF THE SHOOTING

CHAPTER 11

It'd be better for her to be with her friends.

She's just been injured. Let her have a month, some time to get ready.

It's not like she has to return to school immediately. But her friends. She needs to have as normal a life as possible.

She needs to adjust.

She has her whole life to adjust. She needs to be a regular teen girl.

So went the arguments between Mandy's parents when it came to their daughter.

I'd been keeping Mandy what company I could and not out of friendly love. I knew, somehow, that she held the key—that what she had seen needed to be told to Zipper, that he had to listen, had to hear. But in the days leading up to Mandy's abrupt return from the hospital—just a week before she was scheduled to enter a facility that would help her learn how to live life as a paraplegic—she had forgotten about my visitation in her dreams. She had dismissed it as the dreams of a delusional, newly handicapped girl looking for any sign of the life she once knew but might never know again.

"Mandy," I called out.

The only time she almost heard me was when she was dreaming. I took full advantage, trying to share with her the hellish visions of blood, blasts, and limbs that the other Takers had shown to me. But her only visions were full of her and Tom in the days when they used to be a couple. It was always sunny, eerily sunny, and she was always running away from a lengthening shadow. The Taker in me felt the potential nightmare, gravitated towards it, but the dream was Mandy's and as soon as I attempted to set foot in her unconscious, she pulled away.

I next took to showing her signs. I sent pop-ups to her laptop of school shooting articles. Baffled, she just closed them. I tried to text, but I couldn't, so I just sent static on her phone. She just complained about the service and tossed the phone aside.

That's when I saw my opening.

One of the kids in Mrs. Walters' class had written her assigned poem on a card and dropped off a copy for Mandy. After a few lines like "The light of our school is lost" and "Your smile will always be who you are to me," there was a request: "Come to the game."

Mandy tossed the card aside.

She was alone. Her two best friends, Kyla and me, were both gone, and she and Tom had broken up months ago. She was still getting over Tom the night of the accident and spent most her party preparation time trying to find outfits to make him jealous. Now, she worried that he'd never notice her again. He'd make an effort to turn his eyes away if, and when, she returned to school.

That game is the perfect place for her to touch base with her friends.

You want her rolled down in a wheelchair in front of everyone? For her first time out in public?

They want to make her a guest of honor.

For what? Driving in a car with two dead, drunk girls?

She's a part of that school. The kids need to see that she's okay.

Does she look okay to you? Besides, the lawyer said it'd be better if she didn't make any appearances saying she was fine.

Mandy could hear her parents still arguing over what was best for her.

"Nice of you to ask me," she whispered towards the door.

She thought back to a kid who underwent surgery and spent time in a wheelchair. Daryl something or other. Kids were supportive of him. But he needed leg surgery. He didn't get into a car and take someone else's life.

"I'm never going back to that school," Mandy whispered. "I can't."

I fought to show her pictures of her friends, including one where Tom had a gun and had come back from hunting with his dad. But nothing connected.

Mandy just sat there, listening to her parents argue out the rest of her life.

She needed to make a decision, and fast.

That day, Takers were causing accidents left and right.

Two cars ran into each other on White Mountain Road. One was a police officer, Danielson, the one who told my mother that I was dead. The Takers' energy told me that Danielson might've spotted Zipper at the game before he had a chance to open fire. Now, he'd be too busy going back and forth with the other driver and the insurance company.

Another kid, Big Adam, broke his leg. I never knew him. He was a few years out of high school, but judging from his aura, he was the type of guy who might run and tackle a shooter.

Everywhere Takers fluttered, and everywhere they were winning.

A new thought struck me, no doubt inspired by my fellow Takers.

I was a Taker too. Maybe I wasn't here to stop anything. Maybe I was here to take the souls of some of my friends to wherever they needed to go.

Suddenly, a new picture formed before me.

It was Steph, with her long, slightly snarled hair, her vibrant eyes now empty of light.

"Not her," I whispered.

I expected to hear Crazy T taunt me, but he was too busy making sure every detail was perfect. Instead, a hazy black mist, the once human form of Kyla, appeared before me.

"If Zipper doesn't do what's right, Steph will," she told me.

"Impossible," I said.

I stared straight into the dark mass that was my former best friend.

"If there's any humanity left in you, help Mandy," I said.

I hoped to conjure some of that humanity.

Instead, Kyla smirked and then said to me: "Mandy will drink from the same cup we have. She'll be dead before the week is out."

As Kyla faded, taunting me, I felt confused. Was Zipper my best target? Steph? Mandy? I couldn't protect that many kids.

I reached into the darkness, into the Taker within me.

I realized everything Kyla said could be true.

There was very little I could still do, but I had to fight.

My first strike against the Takers was an unexpected one. The day of the shooting, Alex and Steph bumped into each other. It was right before the fourth position class. Alex was lost in texting, and Steph was skimming over a book for a makeup test she couldn't put off any longer. Steph's book dropped, and she started cursing.

"Easy," Alex said.

He put up his free hand as if that would change anything.

"Don't you people ever watch where you're going?" Steph asked.

"What's that supposed to mean?" Alex replied.

"You just crash into whoever you like, don't you, you drunk?" Steph said in accusation.

Alex looked coldly, plainly, and said: "I wasn't in the car."

Steph picked up her own book, muttered: "It'd be better if you were" as she walked away.

Alex followed.

I stood by, watching their aching auras mingle. There was so much volatility there, so much anger, but together their auras held in check.

"That's a real crappy attitude you've got there," Alex said.

Steph turned around. "*I* have the crappy attitude? I wasn't the one who drove his girlfriend to drink."

"Fay had problems when I met her."

"And you just made them worse, didn't you?"

"So it's my fault she got behind the wheel drunk, is that it?" Alex asked.

His voice broke. Steph had hit a nerve.

"She was going to meet some guy at my party," Alex said. "She loved to torture me. We'd broken up. She'd cheated on me, and she still punished *me* for it. Like it was my fault or something."

Steph stood silent, said nothing.

"Maybe I should've thrown some kind of intervention like you see on reality TV. But I was too busy partying. I was a rotten boyfriend, and she was a rotten girlfriend, but that doesn't mean I drove her to it. Hell, I even tried to empty bottles, to get her away from it. That's why she dumped me."

Just then, even Alex's glasses couldn't hide the tremors of pain on his face. Tears flowed freely. He looked around to see if anyone else in the hall noticed. They did. He dried the tears with his sleeve.

"If I never threw that party, everyone would be alive and this nightmare would just disappear," Alex said.

The bell rang, perfectly timed, I might add, like in some teen TV show.

"I have to go," Steph said.

Alex nodded.

Steph started walking.

"What I'm trying to say," Alex said. "I'm trying to say sorry."

Steph's gaze lowered to the hallway. She didn't look down, but she did call back: "It wasn't your fault. It was hers."

Steph kept walking, but then turned around right as Alex headed to his first class.

"And in science class," Steph said, "you touched me. Don't. Not without my permission."

Alex nodded weakly.

But I could see Steph still looking at him.

It was official. Steph fell for Alex. I recognized the light in her eyes. I'd been there before.

"Fight for her," I whispered to Alex as he walked away. "She'll be your chance to be a good boyfriend."

He stopped the moment I said that. I could swear he heard me.

"Just let me go," I said.

Alex said nothing, started walking to class again.

I looked at him as if I was seeing him for the last time. My boyfriend. The love of my short life. How I needed him. How Steph did too.

Right before the next class, Principal Buckley called an emergency assembly in the guise of a pep rally.

The cheerleaders were there, kicking, tossing each other up and down, while the team players were called one by one, even given nicknames like Tom "Night Terror" and Alex "The Annihilator". The cool kids refused to use their last names. It messed up the flow. I laughed at how tough these kids thought they were and reveled in the energy of my friends. It was good to see kids cheering, laughing again, even if my fatal accident was still a cloud over the entire championship game.

Alex reminded anyone who forgot by stepping up and saying, on the microphone, "For Fay."

The crowd roared.

"For Kyla," he added.

Again, there was thunderous applause.

"For Ms. Lynn Carson," Alex added.

The applause ceased the moment the words came out of his mouth.

All eyes turned on Steph, who herself turned around, looking back at the stunned crowd.

The crowd was silent, even though Mr. Higgins and Mrs. Walters attempted to lead the claps and the cheerleaders called out, following the teachers' lead. Some polite applause followed from the kids, at which point Steph got up and walked out, cursing and shaking her head.

Alex followed.

That's when Mr. Buckley took the microphone, attempting to make the save.

"We understand that you guys have a big party planned after school," Mr. Buckley said, "with a bigger party planned tonight. We ask that our players remember their championship game and do the school proud by getting rest."

The crowd booed. The pep rally was breaking apart.

Coach Ryan stepped forward and added, "Any of my players who have even a trace of alcohol on their breath won't be playing."

No one dared to boo the coach. The kids grew quiet.

"We also ask," Mr. Buckley said, "that you remember the show of support you're giving for Fay, Kyla, and Ms. Carson, and that you don't drink at tonight's party. Please remember your friends. We want a safe, dry game tonight."

The booing started up again.

"So that you know, effective immediately, we will have breathalyzers at each game. Franklin Shore is our guest tonight. Let's be hospitable."

The jeers grew so loud Mr. Buckley had to stop.

Coach Ryan hollered and only then did the kids quiet down.

He was shouting a chant, and the kids were picking it up.

"How do you spell soccer?"

"B-u-r-g-u-n-d-y!"

I laughed. Most kids probably didn't know the answer to that one, anyway.

"I can't hear you! How do you spell soccer?"

"B-U-R-G-U-N-D-Y H-I-L-L!"

The chants became louder until only one voice, one pulsing cry, echoed across the gymnasium.

Mr. Buckley then stepped forward to undertake the unenviable task of dismissing the kids back to their classes.

Steph was in the corridor, crying.

Alex kept calling her name, but Steph didn't want to come out.

Her pain pulled me in, but I knew I couldn't help her.

Because of me, a piece of her would be gone for her entire life.

I thought of guiding Alex toward her, but her aura was so distraught, in such reds and dark pinks, that I knew I'd have to play Cupid another time.

Instead, I concentrated on a memory I had of Steph when she was just a girl.

She skipped around, jump roping and counting until she hit one-hundred.

All the girls stood around, watching to see if she could do it.

I was there; Kyla was; Sue, everyone.

When she jumped the rope for the hundredth time, we roared as if we were sending off a queen.

I dropped a hint of a shy guy in the background, Alex. He was so young, such a cute little kid with sloppy, shifting bangs and darting eyes.

I saw Steph smile as she thought of the memory.

She began to grasp that Alex liked her once before, that he might like her once again.

Alex called again for Steph.

She let him walk by. It was too soon.

But through her tears, she smiled.

She picked herself up, dried her eyes, and marched off to her next class.

The drama didn't end there.

Zipper was heading back with his trademark Army green backpack when the soccer players, fresh from the rally, came crashing through.

The less mature groupies, boys who weren't athletic but liked to suck up to the team to get invites to all the cool parties, barreled down the hallway with Tom and a few other players on their shoulders. They hit a few kids good-naturedly but were too caught up in their own hype, knocking into lockers, laughing, then careening down the hall again until Tom's foot took out Zipper. Zipper nearly crashed his knee into the floor, but the soccer players never even looked to see if he was okay. They just kept chanting, singing, roughhousing.

Zipper looked up; it was clear that he didn't exist to them.

They weren't being nasty and bullying him. They just didn't even notice his existence, his presence in the hallway.

When he went down, the mighty soccer players were too good to be bothered to notice.

I shook my head. The memories, the dreams that included some of Zipper's targets, flew out of his aura as if I'd never planted them there. His rage, undeniable, intense, clouded him. And to think—Zipper might have decided on another plan that day. But now his plan, months in the making, was signed and sealed.

One careless foot might lead to the death of players, families, friends.

I did all I could to magnify the auras of the players, to get them to turn around, to say sorry.

Instead, Rope Man stood by the players, tossing his ghostly noose over their necks.

While the soccer team celebrated their awesomeness, the Takers circled around them, celebrating their deaths with images of blood and gore.

I couldn't make it past my fellow Takers.

Zipper rose, checked himself for scratches, cursed, and headed off. A twisted smile took his lips. He was sizing up his prey.

Down in the basement of the school, I spotted Zipper's stash for the first and last time.

He had his own locker since he worked in maintenance after school, and he actually had petrol in the locker along with the ends of broken rakes and chains. Oddly enough, he could make up an explanation for almost anything in the locker. But deeper, down by the school's foundation, he'd actually removed and patched pieces of concrete when his boss was busy drinking and doing nothing.

Zipper had actual bombs planted in the school, right at its foundation, at a time when school security should have made such a thing impossible.

I knew after the soccer team ran Zipper over that I had little chance of winning him over before the game. But if I could make just one of these bombs go off at a time and in a way that would hurt no one, I might be able to save the school. I concentrated, used all of my energy to focus on opening the locker. I planned to ignite the little bit of petrol to do the trick. It was a dangerous game, and if I missed a bomb here or there, I could become the murderer I was trying to stop.

But the locker only rattled. Nothing went off.

I concentrated harder, only to hear clapping by my side.

I saw a blackish rope still around the white neck of an eyeless ghost.

"Bravo," Crazy T said. "Now you're getting into the spirit of things. It's nice to see you becoming a true Taker."

"I'll stop you in whatever way I can."

Crazy T laughed. "You can't even ignite petrol," he said.

"And you can? Prove it."

"Reverse psychology?" Crazy T asked. "How quaint. But don't worry, kid. You'll see exactly what I can do tonight."

"Take me. Leave the rest of the school alone."

"Lame heroics won't help you," Crazy T said. "You took lives just like I did, and you will go to hell for it. But first you'll take my place."

"They're innocent—"

"No one's innocent." Crazy T smirked. "What's the matter? You look so helpless."

I looked at him, trying to figure out how to fight such consuming hatred.

"Here, let me help you out," Crazy T said.

He pointed towards the petrol, started a small explosion. The locker burst just a bit, became tinged with black on the inside. Then the fire consumed itself.

"You heard the explosion, right?" Crazy T asked.

His skeletal finger pointed upstairs, where kids walked between classes.

"All those people and not one of them figured it out," he said. "Go ahead. Feel their auras."

I did. Crazy T was right.

"There's nothing you can do to save these pigs," Crazy T said. "Just get ready to take souls. Just get ready to be a Taker."

With that, Crazy T disappeared, and I felt pulled elsewhere, to an immense grief. I felt pulled towards my mother.

My mother's feet shuffled along the rug of the Bert Thompson, J.D., her court-appointed legal counsel. She'd been surprised by his quick appointment until she learned that my father had put in for a free lawyer immediately. He must've been too drunk to remember. As she waited, she reviewed the day of my death in her mind. It'd be years before my mother would train herself to overcome this one most painful moment of my life. She imagined me shrieking as the jeep crashed into the caravan, imagined the young mother's reaction to her certain and sudden death. I felt more afraid of reliving my death in my mother's aura than I did thinking of how it actually happened several nights ago.

"Ms. DeSoto?" the lawyer asked, coming out to greet my mom. "I'm Bert."

Mom rose, shook Bert's hand solemnly.

"I was referred by—"

"Kirk contacted me when he found out about your financial issues. I was permitted to step in." Bert looked around. "Is Mr. DeSoto here?"

"His name's not DeSoto."

"Is your ex-husband here?"

"He chose not to be here today. It's just me."

"Why, may I ask? The lawsuit's going to be against both of you."

"He's aware of that. He's just...he has a drinking problem."

"I see."

Bert escorted my mother into the office.

They sat down quietly.

"I've read the police reports and first, I'd like to extend my sympathies, Ms. DeSoto."

"Thank you."

"I can't imagine the burden of getting a lawyer so soon after..."

"What choice did I have?"

Bert shrugged, looked over the case files.

"So, am I going to have to pay money I can't afford? Can you be honest with me, Mr. Thompson?"

The lawyer looked up from the files, looked at a spot away from my mother, thinking.

"Are you aware your daughter lost her license?" Bert asked.

My mother looked down, then answered, "Not before I was served. Fay—my daughter—she must have gone through the mail."

"That complicates things," Bert said.

"But didn't Mandy get in the car willingly?" Mom asked. "Isn't it just as much her fault?"

Mr. Thompson slid over some papers. "Just got these this morning," he said.

My mother looked at them, nearly dropped the file.

"The victim's family is suing too?" she asked. Her voice nearly shattered. "Mr. Thompson, I'm not made of money."

"Do you own your house?" the lawyer asked.

My mother gulped, tried to make sure she heard the question right.

"I do," she said. "I mean, the mortgage isn't paid off yet, but I have years of equity built up."

"And how much do you make a year?"

"50K last year. Why?"

Bert Thompson took a moment. "Ms. DeSoto, I'm not going to lie to you. You have a drunken daughter and Kirk tells me you admitted that you looked the other way."

Mom started sniffling, but nodded.

"She lost her license, and you didn't even know," Bert added. "Then she crashed your car. Her father lives in another state and can't even make his appointments because he's an alcoholic. Ms. DeSoto, the judge will decide, not me, but the case does not look promising."

"What can I do?" Mom asked, helplessly.

"Don't call Mrs. Bilki again," he told her, "and don't say a word to anyone about the case unless I okay it."

Mom nodded.

"How much can I lose?" she asked.

"Does your husband have a house?"

My mother shook her head.

"A job?" Bert asked.

She shook her head again.

Mr. Thompson fiddled with his papers and said, "Ms. DeSoto, you need to survive. They can't take that away from you. Everything else, that's for a judge to decide."

My mother stared out the window.

Alive, I'd cost her college.

Dead, I'd cost her everything.

A new grief pulled me closer. Mandy waved her arms in bed. She liked the movement, the free motion of her arms, a freedom her legs would never again know. This time, another bright card fluttered from her hands to the floor.

"Come to the game, Mandy. We all want to see you!"

— Signed,

Sue

It was meant to be a gesture of finality towards her former life, to the kids of Burgundy Hill High.

But the card brought something emotional to mind: me. Mandy thought back to the times we skipped class, talking about life issues in the bathroom over a drink or two. She thought back to when we first became drinking buddies and to the few times we got high together. She was wondering if her life would've been better if we never got close in high school. It might have been.

But *might have been* was now as dead as I was.

In that brief flicker of thought, Mandy remembered something.

She was standing in bright light, standing with me. Only it wasn't me. It was my ghost. She thought of how awful I looked dead, black and pulpy, like a bleeding pen. She asked herself: *And what was with her head?* The thought of that being me scared her, and as she lay in her room, waiting to move to her new treatment facility, she remembered something else. There were words. Feelings. Like half-remembered dreams from weeks ago.

But this was no dream, she insisted. *This was real.*

She immediately dismissed the thought.

Yet, there was this image of me, black and alive, muttering words of danger, words of urgency, words she just couldn't remember.

If it's true, she thought, *move that card.*

I sensed her message; messages to me came loud and clear in her aura.

"I don't know if I can," I said.

Still, at that moment, I didn't have to.

A breeze fluttered. The card moved. Mandy was lying stunned, watching.

Gotta love all too unlikely coincidences, especially when they suit you.

I smiled; Mandy didn't. She simply shook her head, as if shaking the thoughts of me away.

I moved closer, started whispering back the memories of our old conversation.

"Fay," she called back.

"Yes?"

"What's the afterlife like?"

"There is a heaven and a hell," I had said. *"There's just two groups of teens and kids waiting to get to one or the other."*

"Are you going to heaven now?" she asked me.

"That spot goes to you," I had said.

Mandy lied there a long while. I nearly gave up projecting the images into her aura until I saw her head roll to its side and heard her say, "That spot goes to you."

A tear formed in the corner of her right eye.

"Fay, what have you done to me?" she asked. "It was always like you to avoid responsibility until the very end."

I spoke in images through her aura again.

She remembered, if vaguely.

"You're not taking her..." a voice like mine declared.

"We won't have to," another voice said.

Mandy felt me around her, recalled the feeling of protection that she had in just that moment.

She started to cry.

I could feel her aura shifting, could sense her shutting down, tuning me out.

Just then, an image came to mind: I was there, a black mist, and she was there, herself, only in a hospital robe.

All I need you to know right now...

She was thinking it, mumbling the words.

But the image didn't quite connect.

"Why can't I just walk again?" Mandy asked herself.

The words, the image, both were so close, but now so far gone. Mandy was lamenting her own obstacles now, and there was no room for anyone else. For a moment, I was in her heart again, but now I was gone.

"I just want to go one day without thinking of you," she said to herself. "One day without being reminded, every day, of one horrible night out."

You can't forget, I told her. *Not yet.*

Her aura sensed the urgency, but not the words.

Mandy rolled over, fluttered her arms, and then looked at her legs.

She then picked up the remote and started to watch way too much TV.

"Maybe I'll go," she said, thinking of the game. "Maybe not."

The school day ended with Mrs. Walters. She taught a mandatory reading workshop during study hall to kids whose English grades dropped significantly since progress reports. She had just assigned the memoir *Please Stop Laughing At Me* by Jodee Blanco despite serious reservations.

It had been on the curriculum for years, and its folded light covers with a young Jodee showed as much when the students crinkled the copies in their hands. Once upon a time, the English / Reading and Life Education departments jointly adopted the title as a warning against the dangers of bullying and alienation.

Tonight, it was to become just another sad irony.

Mrs. Walters had tossed and turned in bed the night before when deciding whether to change the book. A few parents had called, complained about some of the more memorable scenes in the memoir. And Mrs. Walters wasn't at all partial to a scene in the book where Jodee cut her face with glass or a rather disturbing poem that she wasn't sure kids this year needed to read.

"We can order another book," she told the class as she described Jodee's struggles.

"Why?" Tom asked.

He was so pumped with testosterone for the big game.

Mrs. Walters thought back to Jodee along with a word Tyler, Jodee's big crush, signed in her yearbook.

"I think maybe you kids have seen even more than Jodee in the past month," Mrs. Walters answered honestly.

"And it's not like we have a bullying problem in sad little Burgundy Hill," Sue said.

Mrs. Walters tried not to smirk at Sue's ignorance. She put on her best professional face and said, "Bullying is a problem everywhere."

"You have to say that, don't you?" Tom asked. "I mean, I don't get why they have all those stupid laws. Maybe some kids need to learn how to take a joke."

Zipper, who *just* started getting lower grades, sat in the class, staring straight ahead. He was too busy reviewing everything in his mind to get much out of the lesson.

"Why don't we put it to a class vote?" Sue said. "Whoever wants to read about a whiny girl getting hit with concrete, raise your hand."

"I don't think that's Jodee's main point, Sue," Mrs. Walters said, "and I'd appreciate it if you were a bit more sensitive."

"I'm sensitive," Sue said. "Once, when my pet turtle died, I cried for like *two* whole hours."

"You killed that turtle," Tom told her. "You sat right on the shell. You wanted to see if it would support your weight. It didn't."

"Shut up," Sue told him.

"I can see the sensitivity shining through the classroom," Mrs. Walters said.

Usually, Mrs. Walters didn't like sarcasm in the classroom. With the kids in this class, she couldn't always help it, though. It had become too much of a survival skill.

"Please raise your hands if you feel comfortable reading this book," Mrs. Walters said.

Nearly every hand went up. Zipper's hand didn't.

"Please raise your hand if you'd rather read something else."

"Like what?" Sue asked.

"*Shakespeare Made Fun*," Mrs. Walters said.

The hands stayed down.

"John," Mrs. Walters said. "Your hand didn't go up."

"It's Zipper," Zipper told her.

"Sorry, Zipper," Mrs. Walters said. "Do you have any thoughts on this issue?"

Zipper looked around the classroom. Each kid had a number on them, in his mind. Tom was one of the kids who'd get shot first. He was turned around, the whole class was, watching Zipper, who was seated in the back. He was just so creepy. Even teachers sensed something was wrong and placed him in the back of the room.

"Doesn't matter to me," Zipper said. "I'm not going to read the book, anyway."

The class laughed.

"Loser," Sue called back.

She was quiet enough to think she avoided detection, but the class, of course, was quiet at just that moment, magnifying her whisper.

"Apologize," Mrs. Walters told Sue.

Sue looked back half-heartedly, not even catching Zipper's eyes, and muttered a sarcastic: "I'm really sorry."

"I bet your father is too," Zipper said. "If he just stayed sober and away from your mom that night..."

The class, sensitive as they were, roared.

Sue swore at Zipper, who sat with a nasty smirk on his face.

Mrs. Walters looked at Zipper, stunned.

She then started to phone the office. Zipper stood up.

"That was uncalled for. I'm sorry, Sue," he said. "You have no idea how sorry I am."

Sue just stared icily at Zipper. She did have the good sense to apologize for swearing, though.

Mrs. Walters put the phone down, wrote up two detention slips instead.

"You have until Tuesday afternoon to serve," she said, handing over the slips.

Class went on, and Zipper sat there, planning.

He'd been careless. He wouldn't be again. Nothing must get in the way of the plan. Nothing.

⁓

Just after school, Mr. Peterson had Zipper cleaning the bleachers one more time before the big game.

Zipper had to make sure there were no disgusting patches of filth after the morning rain, and he was an adviser to the one man who could call the game off if the field was too wet.

"Well," Mr. Peterson asked. "What do you think?"

"Wet, but playable," Zipper said.

"You sure? If one preppy breaks his neck—"

"They'll be safe, at least as safe as they can be."

"What the hell's that supposed to mean?"

"Soccer's a dangerous game."

Mr. Peterson chuckled. "Football's a dangerous game. If you ask me, tackling a few of these kids might do them good. Soccer's too...gentle."

"It's a sport of skill. Like checkers moving around on a field. I admire it. All it lacks is a hunter."

"Like you've done a day of exercise in your life." Mr. Peterson took a drink out of a concealed container, then asked Zipper: "You planning to show tonight?"

"Why?"

"Principal Buckley wants someone on the field in case he needs 'em."

"For what? Mowing?"

"To keep the fields clear during the game."

"I'm not a bouncer."

"Rumor is there may be a storm coming."

"Do you melt in the rain or something?"

"Don't be a prick. I have to pick my girls up from their own games."

"I see."

"So can you make it?"

Zipper wore his trademark smirk. "Wouldn't miss it," he said.

"Good. Be here at five o'clock." Mr. Peterson took another swig and then added: "You can leave now. Rest up. I'll finish the bleachers."

Zipper nodded, walked off, but looked back. The exact placement of everyone from Alex and Tom's families, to Mrs. Walters, to Sue, to their soccer groupies, unfolded before him. He could picture the surest way to ignite the explosives, and he knew just when to take out his gun. He walked along the woods, plotting his escape route, and then laughed.

There was only one escape Zipper wanted and only one thing that could provide it: a gun, carefully hidden.

Sure enough, my friends decided to start the party early. I'd never realized just how much we drank until I was there with them, watching beer can after beer can pile up.

How I longed for the taste, even the aftertaste, of just one can of beer.

But now I got to see, for the first time, sober, just what my friends acted like.

There were dozens of people there. Some, like Jessica, drank moderately and didn't attract much attention. The one who stood out to me was Sue. She was trying to draw a sexy tattoo on some guy she picked up just before they made out. She finished and laughed drunkenly. She started making out way too wildly with this guy who just followed her to a mall and gave her his number. That was the qualification: some older guy showed interest, and Sue was willing to compromise every last moral just to make out with him and have a boyfriend. Alcohol was the means of loosening her up.

"Careful, Sue," Tom said. "They'll never let you in if you can't walk in a straight line."

"You can't play a straight line," Alex said, "but they let you on the team."

Both Alex and Tom drank—stupidly—before the game. They told themselves it was just one beer, which they savored, and that was true. It wasn't as if they were making themselves the entertainment the way that Sue was. But they couldn't go without that one beer.

"I'll bet you," Tom said, "that I make more goals than you."

"You're on. But what's the wager? Make it worth my time."

Tom smirked and then looked at Sue. "Ten minutes with Sue," he said.

"I can get that for free," Alex replied.

"Hey," Sue said.

Her boyfriend stood up, trying to make a stand, but he was too drunk and fell down again.

Alex sipped his beer, looking away from it all.

For a moment, his eyes became clear, alert, and he looked right at me. I'd forgotten that I was there at all.

"Fay," he whispered.

There I was, the queen of black mist, which was the ghostly equivalent of letting your boyfriend see you without your makeup on.

I had one moment, one clear second, when I could tell Alex how much I loved him, how sorry I was for everything. Or I could tell him how much danger he was in.

I pointed to a zipper, the only thing that came to mind.

"Damn," Alex said. "I could've sworn I just saw Fay."

"Knock it off with that garbage. We have a game," Tom said.

"She pointed to a zipper," Alex said.

Tom and Sue laughed, as did Sue's drunken boyfriend, who probably didn't know why.

"That's sick," Tom said. "You have the hots for a dead girl."

"Not *my* zipper," Alex said.

"Then whose?"

"Sue's."

"So Ghost Fay has the hots for Sue?" Tom asked. "Did you drive her to it?"

"Stop talking about Fay," Alex said.

"Fine. Just keep your mind on the game, you drunk." Tom came over, gave Alex a pat on the shoulder and said, "Let's go. It's showtime."

The two clanged their beer cans together and then tossed them. They brushed the alcohol from their mouths and then gathered their gear. Drunken kids, led by Sue, stood up and cheered the great soccer team's departure like it was a military triumph in ancient Rome.

I looked over Zipper's shoulder one more time as he texted away, typing on his Twitter feed with no followers.

"This is my last time on Twitter," he tweeted.

He tweeted a few smaller messages, like: "When police discover this it'll be too late," and "This was done out of love, not hate" and "Love you, Mom and Pop" with a link to "Adam's Song" by Blink 182 to stress how it wasn't his parents' fault.

How lonely the posts looked on the web. Zipper's blog had already announced his suicide, and no one had noticed.

THE NIGHT OF THE
SHOOTING

CHAPTER 12

Phantoms of white light, shaped like butterflies and orbs, swirled around me. I was too consumed in darkness to see their faces.

"Belinda?" I asked.

Three of the spirits came up to me. One was Belinda, with the glowing white-blond hair. The other two I didn't know or couldn't make out, Taker that I was.

"You will not fight without friends," Belinda said to me.

"That's a little vague," I said. "How many of you are going to stand by me?"

"By you?" Belinda said. "None."

"You might want to look up the meaning of the word *friends*, then."

"Such a Taker," Belinda said. "So negative."

"I'm fighting so that the rest of my school doesn't end up like me, young and dead. I'd say that gives me the right to be a little negative."

"That's not your fight," Belinda said. "This you *must* understand. You cannot save the entire school. Your fight is with Crazy T, who will test you as his successor. In that fight, you must stand alone. Our fight is for the lives of your friends."

I looked around at the mists of Takers filling the skies. There were so many, circling, each ready to claim a life.

"I'll take whatever help I can get," I said, "wherever it comes from."

A ghostly red fiery lake opened up, surrounding and then swallowing the field of play. The Burgundy Hill High fields became like a supernatural pit of hell, with Takers flying everywhere.

The players for both teams were out on the field, passing balls, making plays, warming up for the biggest, and perhaps last, game of their lives.

Spectators began settling in, filling the stands, including Mrs. Walters, who took to the ticket stand.

Next were the families of Alex, Tom, and the other players. They were a loud, rowdy bunch, and they staked out the best seats, competing with the Franklin Shore families to see who got preferential seating.

Steph showed up alone. She hid in the bleachers with a few familiar high school students and said little.

Sue and Jessica and the drunks came next, hoping to sneak in without having to take the breathalyzer. But Mr. Higgins was there with Mr. Buckley. Neither was that capable of administering the test, but test Sue they did. Not too surprisingly, Sue and her friends cheated the system and passed. Leave it to Sue—the one time being a drunk might save her life and she had to play it sober.

"This will be a good thing for the school," Mr. Buckley said, turning his attention away from the drinkers.

He always spoke like he was before a crowd, even if he was just speaking to himself.

"We've dedicated the game to Fay, Kyla, Mandy, and to Steph and to Steph's mother," Mr. Buckley went on to anyone who'd listen. "We've asked each of the parents to be here."

"Have any accepted?" Mr. Higgins asked.

Mr. Buckley shook his head. "It's too soon," he said. "I do hope someone shows up to say a few words to the crowd first. These kids need a boost."

The crowd grew in size and in noise, until nearly the entire town of Burgundy Hill found itself crammed into the bleachers by the lights.

I looked at the field. Takers were following the soccer stars, mocking them.

Rope Man, at home in his native jock element, tossed a lasso across the neck of Tom, who he planned to personally see killed. Burn Girl and Cut Girl took stations near where Zipper had loaded up the explosives underground, just waiting for the time to detonate it all. Perhaps the most sickening sight was Kyla, who followed Alex around more overtly than she did in life, smiling as she planned to stake her claim. I saw her attention shift just a moment, and then I saw why: unbelievably, Mandy was wheeling herself to just beside the bleachers. Her parents followed. Kyla smiled her Taker smile, extended her arms, welcoming Mandy to death by fire.

"Each Taker only gets to take one soul," Crazy T said.

He was fluttering among the legions of black mists, then swooped right down by Mrs. Walters.

"I know just who I'm going for," Crazy T went on.

"Be strong," Belinda told me.

"If every Taker gets one soul," I said, "then I know just who I'm going for, too."

Crazy T sized me up. "Try it," he said.

"All in good time."

The Takers took their positions, forming impenetrably around the explosives, around the soccer team, and around Zipper, who was wandering around the sides of the fields with his green camouflage backpack. Moments earlier, Takers clouded him so much that not even I could see through that much darkness. I could only imagine him loading his guns, checking them in the woods, making perfectly sure that nothing would go wrong. I could feel the anger, the fear, in his aura, which whipped around in angry reds and blacks like a bloody tiger unleashed upon the crowd. Up and down, Zipper paced to calm himself, using the pretense of having to check the field.

Before the soccer team was announced, out came the cheerleaders.

"How do you spell champion?" the captain asked a live crowd.

She was a demure redhead named Monica, who stood in perfect place by her teammates. I wondered if she knew I had died at all.

"B-U-R-G-U-N-D-Y H-I-L-L!" her squad shouted, jumping up and down and cheering wildly.

The soccer moms and dads clapped, but the crowd, unappeased, started their own chants.

"On the first day, God made soccer," Sue's drunken boyfriend shouted, "and saw that it was great."

The high school boys took the lead.

"On the second day," they continued, "God made Franklin Shore soccer. We all make mistakes."

The boys laughed and chanted "We all make mistakes" again, as if it was ridiculously funny. Alcohol made idiots feel like Oscar Wilde, I suppose. I should know. I spent my life as one of them.

Another bench, filled with equally drunk Franklin Shore kids, took to chanting "Sucks" every time the cheerleaders spelled out Burgundy Hill.

This chant led to parents cringing, and a few chant leaders got broken up by teachers.

The gesture was unnecessary, though, as the entire field became quiet the moment Mandy wheeled into full view.

A huge ovation started out and soon the Burgundy Hill chants turned to: "We love you, Mandy!" The Franklin Shore boys even took to the chants, and the parents and other students were silent, just watching the only survivor of the most infamous drunk driving crash in town history situate herself next to the bleachers.

Principal Buckley made a big production out of going up to Mandy, shaking her hand like she was a visiting ambassador from some far-off country.

In a way, I suppose she was, having been to death and back again.

Crazy T sought my attention, forming from the darker mists with a cruel smile on his lips as he floated, stirring up his Takers.

I stood by Mandy, as did a few Keepers, trying to give her strength.

"We don't want to make any speeches," Mandy's mom said.

"I'll say a few words," Mandy volunteered.

"Dear, no," her father said. "No one expects—"

"I should say something," Mandy said. "Is Steph here?" she asked.

Principal Buckley nodded.

"Okay. Get me a mic," she said.

Principal Buckley went back to the crowd and tried to quiet the chants. The chants of "Mandy" only grew louder until everyone was on their feet, applauding. Principal Buckley went over to the announcer's table and asked them to announce that Mandy had something to say. They did so and passed the principal a working mic. He passed it along to Mandy, whose parents wheeled her to the center of the field.

Mandy looked around. The two teams were getting ready to take their announce positions to be called out to the field, but not one of them was focused on hearing their names. They all stood, applauding, waiting for Mandy to speak.

"One week ago," Mandy said, "I was in a wreck that claimed three lives."

All applause died; there wasn't a sound on the field or in the bleachers.

"My best friend, Fay, is dead. My good friend Kyla is gone, and Steph's mom, who was innocent, is gone, too."

Mandy started crying, but still there was silence.

"I learned this week that I may be in a wheelchair for the rest of my life, and I grew scared and angry and wished that I was dead," Mandy said. "But what we did was wrong. My parents don't want me to say anything because of a lawsuit. We need the money, since it will take millions and millions to keep me alive for the rest of my life. But at least I'm alive. Steph's mom isn't. And while I can't ever apologize enough for what I did, for what Fay did, and for what Kyla did, as the only one of us left to speak, I feel I should say sorry from the bottom of my heart. I need to warn other kids not to drink and drive the way I did. I know that sounds corny. I know you'll do what you'll do anyway, and I can even tell a few of my friends have been drinking before this game. Some of them got behind the wheel. But if one kid looking at me, seeing a reminder of what drinking can do, if that kid stops, then all of this will have been worth it, everything except the deaths that didn't have to happen. I'm not a great speaker, and I don't know quite how to end," Mandy said, "but I will fight to be back in high school before graduation. I want to be a daily reminder to my friends to stay sober. And I want to be a daily reminder of how precious life is and of how quickly it can be taken away."

Mandy handed the microphone to Principal Buckley as an awkward applause broke through the bleachers.

Mandy's parents wheeled her back to where she was, and Alex and Tom, the two captains of the soccer team, came to take the mic.

The cheers were immediate.

"A week ago, we lost two great friends and a great mom," Alex said once the cheers died down. "We want to dedicate this game to them."

"Burgundy Hill is a family," Tom added. "Every goal we score—"

"—If Tom scores any," Alex interjected.

The crowd forced a small laugh, if only to break up the awkwardness of the moment.

"We dedicate each goal to Steph, to her mom, to Fay, to Kyla, and to everywhere here," Tom concluded.

The applause increased as Principal Buckley turned the mic over to the announcers, who asked for a final, sweeping round of applause. The crowd obliged. The announcers then indicated that it was time to call the two teams.

Zipper stood there, surrounded by Takers. I don't know if an ounce of the emotion on the field or in the bleachers made it to him. His face was blank as he stood to the side, backpack now in hand, simply waiting.

I focused on making myself appear.

The energy it took would be enormous, but if I could just appear to Zipper the way I must have to Alex, if I could just let him know that I knew, that I cared, then maybe the lives of my friends would be spared.

"Help me," I said to the Keepers floating around as I mustered all my energy.

I felt my dark energy, still full of anger and pain at my death, growing instead.

A supernatural storm circled overhead and manifested itself in storm clouds that even the spectators of the living world could see hovering over the fields.

"We're sorry," Belinda told me. "We have to use our energy for one purpose and one purpose only: to keep the bombs from exploding. You must face the Takers on your own. Use your strength."

I did my best to quickly fly by and call out to Alex, to Mandy, to Zipper, to any who might see me, but it was clear that the vortex of Taker energy was too powerful.

The Takers are hungry, I said to myself.

I knew they wouldn't be full until they were glutted on the souls of the living.

In the midst of all this chaos, the announcers started calling the soccer players to the field.

"First up, for Franklin Shore, is #5, ranked 3rd in the state, team starter Will Coldon!"

The crowd either roared or applauded politely before hearing the Burgundy Hill lineup.

"At #7," the announcer said before the crowd went wild.

Even grown men and women were screaming wildly, like Taylor Swift was before them or something.

"He is The Annihilator—"

I didn't hear the rest of Alex's intro over the shouting, but was struck by the irony of The Annihilator so close to his own annihilation. Over the feverish cries, I heard the Takers planning their assault right as the game geared up.

"If he blows up both sets of bleachers first," Kyla told Crazy T, "they won't have anywhere left to run."

"I want to see Lisa bathe in blood," Crazy T said. "He shoots her first."

"She's positioned too far away," Rope Man told him. "Let him shoot the players first. It'll bring more people to the field. Then he can have his way with them."

"We should've waited until we had two shooters," Burn Girl said. "It would've been easy to divide and conquer. But you chose a loner."

"Just see to it that the bombs go off," Crazy T told Burn Girl. "Use as many Takers as you need. The explosion is the only way to guarantee everyone dies. Zipper is just my entertainment. I get him to shoot who I want when I want."

I didn't hear any more Taker bickering. Instead, I saw legions of Takers coordinating to assault the Keepers. The Keepers vowed to keep their place by the bombs. I knew that would be the last stand of this battle.

What I didn't know was how to take Crazy T down. The Takers were just too many and too powerful, and I could feel Zipper losing patience. He might snap at any moment.

Crazy T smirked when he saw something. Steph's aura was also out of control. Her vaunting reds and blacks looked nearly as angry as Zipper's aura. Now I knew why Crazy T let Mandy speak without making any effort to stop her. Steph's anger would get the better of her.

"Drop a gun near the girl," Crazy T said. "Then tempt her. Tempt her to shoot Mandy in the fray, to finish the job Fay started. If Zipper fails, focus on her."

"She's too good a girl," Cut Girl said. "It'll never work."

"Just look at her aura," Crazy T said. "Do it before she calms down. The rest of you—make sure she has a path to the girl in the wheelchair."

The reds and blacks merged with the storm clouds. Steph was close to the edge.

I knew I had to be near, that I had to protect her. I didn't know how. The Taker power, anger, depression, aggression, hatred, and pain filled me. I tried to keep my soul clear, to remember the ways of the Keepers, of insight, protection, and love, but I was a Taker, and the forces around me were too much.

"Stop fighting what you are," Belinda told me. "Use your Taker impulses to your advantage."

"No," I said. "I'm Fay. I'm not just some Taker."

I fought the impulses, fought to hold on to the last shreds of human life, of compassion, of what made me Fay. But as I looked at Belinda's pleading ghostly eyes, I knew it wouldn't be enough.

"Fay died," Belinda said. "Only a Taker remains."

The words, felt so deeply inside my soul, hit me. I had to give in to hold out. I started by letting the Taker energy, Taker thought, the darkness of The Flow, fill me. Crazy T's plan became apparent. He'd kill enough to earn himself a spot in hell. First the bombs. Then the shooting. His best moment: Mrs. Walters, gunned down, along with the older brothers of Alex and Tom, star soccer players in Crazy T's day. Steph was just a diversion to him.

I knew then that Steph and Mandy were the key. They were the two girls Crazy T hadn't counted on, that he didn't believe could even be persuaded to attend the game. They would be my wild cards. If I could use their anger, their depression, their darker energies like a Taker would, I might be able to position them in all the chaos, use them to thwart the efforts of Zipper and Crazy T while the Keepers kept the bombs and explosives at bay.

Right now, I knew that Steph's dark energy was joining with the Taker cloud. I pushed that energy towards the advancing storm clouds to start a downpour.

The Takers knew I was up to something obstructive. Their attack: a temporal one. They played with time, freezing and then propelling it forward until we were in the game. Just when I positioned myself by Steph, they moved time backward, then forward again, until I knew that it was all just one last trick. There'd have to be a moment when Zipper got up, when he whipped the detonator and gun out of his backpack. That would be what I'd watch for, no matter how much Crazy T and his legions played with time.

Time moved back to the moment the game started up. Black cumulonimbus clouds festered overhead, initially unleashing a few large drops, then steady streams of rain.

Meanwhile, the coaches looked towards where Zipper stood.

"Play the game," Zipper said.

"Like hell, kid," Franklin Shore's Coach Derriza said. "Where's Mr. Peterson?"

Zipper pulled out his phone. The coach took it, mumbled a few words, and then handed the phone back. The coach nodded.

Neither coach was willing to let the championship go, to be the first to cave. They ordered their starters to take the line. To rounds of cheers, the players took the field and positioned themselves.

It was Tom starting out against Will of Franklin Shore. Both looked a little jittery; this was the key moment that would decide the tempo of the start of the game. A whistle sounded, and the ball went to Franklin Shore. This Will was a master of control. He maneuvered the ball away from Burgundy Hill's defensive midfielder as he somehow managed to eye his teammates and see where the best place to send the ball was. He decided on a lanky guy, #25, last name Huele, and passed the ball to him. The whole audience felt a subdued silence as Huele passed the ball on and Will came down behind the defender to take the kick. He had such force behind the kick that the ball nearly tore through the goal post, but it did not make the net. This was championship soccer, all right. It was no game for wimps.

Just then, the rains hit. I kept my attention focused on Zipper's aura. He clearly didn't feel rushed despite the downpour.

The field got wet almost immediately. Players were sloshing along, slipping, staining their shin guards, falling in the field.

At this, Zipper smiled. It would make his prey that much easier to trap. He just sat back and let the players wear themselves out.

Will slipped, and Alex went for the ball. Alex moved slower than most of the other players, but maintained his balance. Alex maneuvered closer to the goal than he had any right to be off of a single play, but waiting by the goal were #8 and #27, who drove Alex away from the goal, to the sidelines. No one else from Burgundy Hill could make it far enough in time, so Alex took a wild kick. The kick was easily caught by the goalie, #12, who kicked the ball back into play, but Alex's daring matched Will's tempo. In a game like this, where the kids would have a better match playing water polo, all risks were fair.

A few Keepers kept working over the coaches. Takers went to intercept, but the light of the Keepers kept them at bay.

Suddenly, Burgundy Hill's Coach Ryan called out to Franklin Shore's Coach Derriza.

Zipper's face turned even paler than usual.

"Miguel," Coach Ryan said. "What do you say we call it? Neither set of boys is going to get a decent shot today."

Coach Derriza had played pro *futbol* down in South America, over in Europe, and was the best living player to come out of the area since Coach Ryan played for the last championship Burgundy Hill team. Coach Derriza had played in all kinds of weather, but even he wondered if this was the real way to win a championship.

Coach Derriza looked up and examined the cloud cover. Takers fluttered everywhere, trying to reflect as much sunlight as they could.

"Just give them the first half," Coach Derriza said. "It looks like the clouds are breaking up."

At those words, the Takers stole my play and concentrated on the rain. Puddles started forming over the field and quickly turned to little bogs.

Not one player complained, though, and the crowds cheered them towards the wettest championship soccer game in Burgundy Hill's history. Just then, thunder roared and lightning took the sky. Hail began falling, and part of the crowd grew restless.

Zipper saw his cue. He quietly unzipped his bag and took out both the detonator and an assault rifle.

Crazy T personally protected his protégé so that it was dark out and people were busying themselves covering up from the hail. Many of their auras showed that they were ready to bolt from the bleachers. Zipper waited one more second while Alex tripped in a puddle and fell. The rain, thunder, hail, and lightning made visibility low. Zipper was ready to aim his rifle right for Alex without anyone seeing him quickly enough. I stood in front of Alex, trying to protect him. I tried to appear one last time before Zipper, to change his course, but his mind was made up. Takers swarmed around him, ready to swoop in for the dead as Zipper aimed right for Alex's head and shot. I did what I could to use whatever control of energy I had to make Alex slip. He did, just as the bullet went in his left leg.

The starters and midfielders concentrated on the ball, but Tom was able to signal to Coach Ryan that Alex wasn't getting up. A few Burgundy Hill players huddled around their fallen captain.

Just then, a blinding light came from the bleachers. I knew why. I turned around and saw the Keepers under attack from swarms of Takers. Several Keepers were hauled away by the dark ghosts, but like a Roman legion in the history books, the Keepers bunkered down. Their light grew to blind the Takers, but one person wasn't so moved.

"Now," Crazy T yelled to Zipper.

Zipper held the detonator in his hand. He paused a moment. I could feel his conflict. Still, the good in him had eroded too far away. Kyla took advantage of the situation and used her fury to conjure the lightning. It started striking down. Zipper, the opportunist, pressed down on the detonator. The left bleachers exploded and came toppling down just as the lightning struck.

The Keepers held their line, though, and contained as much of the explosion as they could. Only a few people broke anything, but at least forty people were buried under debris and were crying and screaming.

"One more explosion," I said to myself, "and the whole school will blow away, fields included."

Coach Ryan focused on Alex, but I used a glimmer of light to distract him long enough for the coach to see a second chunk of bleachers fall.

"Lightning struck the bleachers," Coach Ryan called out. "Get everyone off the field!"

Coach Derriza joined him, signaling his players with a wave of his arms. "Game's over," he called to the Franklin Shore boys. "Help get the people out of the debris!"

Lightning still struck down on the poles as the Takers and Keepers took to all-out war in the skies. Takers collided mid-air with the Keepers, many of whom used their light to go right through the Takers and tear them apart. Wisps of mist and light fell back into The Flow, which now hovered like a giant funnel above the fields.

Burn Girl and Cut Girl used their energy to fuel the larger explosion, but Belinda took both Takers out before they could cause more than one tiny dud of a bomb to blow. If anything, Burn Girl and Cut Girl did the crowd a favor as they began to piece together that this wasn't simply a lightning strike. Both Takers burned in their own fiery mists and fell to The Flow.

"Get the kids out of here! It's a bomb," I yelled again and again, until one soccer mom intuitively heard me and took to the chant.

Unfortunately, two Takers, Rope Man and Kyla, attacked me just after the alarm sounded.

"Keep her from me," Crazy T called out.

I used whatever powers I had to flip and twirl, kicking at Rope Man, then dangling the end of his noose and pushing him towards The Keepers. Two Keepers then took Rope Man out.

"Leave her to me," Kyla told Crazy T.

"Kyla," I said. "Rethink this. These are your friends. Help me to help them!"

"I told you—I won't be the only one whose life is cut short."

Her eyes were volcanic red, unnaturally evil. She jumped up and whirled her body around. The motion created massive waves of anger that fed the other Takers, who swooped in and ripped a score of the Keepers in half.

"I could beat you senseless when we were alive," I told Kyla, "and I can do the same now that we're dead."

"Try it."

I formed my own violent ball of mist, which emanated intuitively from my own anger. Takers swirled around it, attempting to have their fill, before I hurled it into Kyla. She braced herself in mid-air, fighting to absorb the ball of darkness, but it was too dark for even her deformed, ghostly body to contain. It blew right through her.

"Loser," she said.

She used what she could of the Taker mists around her and formed black lightning bolts, which she hurled at me as if she was some deranged Zeus from on high.

I weaved in and out of the fellow Takers. Each bolt that hit its target turned the Taker into a mist that was swallowed whole by The Flow. The abyss opened up before me. I could see that the funnel was feeding souls to hell.

As I bobbed and weaved for my supernatural life, Zipper was in full assault mode. He shot at both sets of players, who scrambled for cover. Tom was the boldest. He dove over Alex, trying to protect him. Zipper caught Tom's face in his sights and shot. Fighting as I was, I couldn't make it in time. The bullet hit Tom's face, and he went down by Alex, who screamed. Zipper laughed, eerily, sounding more like Crazy T. I saw why. Crazy T entered his body and possessed him. Zipper shot down as many players as he could before Coach Ryan tackled him. Coach Ryan trembled as he saw the red in Zipper's eyes, and the Takers protected their master by helping Zipper hurl Coach Ryan towards the bleachers. Coach Derizza also fought, but was gunned down by Zipper before the coach could restrain him. The soccer players froze for a moment. Then a group of Franklin Shore and Burgundy Hill players broke off. The Franklin Shore guys distracted Crazy T, putting their lives on the line, while the Burgundy Hill players came around, seeking the element of surprise.

"Jocks never do get any smarter," Crazy T said through Zipper.

Zipper turned and shot down the squad that approached from the side before shooting down the Franklin Shore players who put their lives at risk. The bullets didn't kill them all yet, though. Crazy T, who was now clearly in control, enjoyed hearing the cries and screams of pain. He shot into the players, into the crowd, taking special pleasure in bringing a begging Sue to her knees only to shoot her dead.

Jessica, who cowered by the fallen bleachers, tried not to scream. At the behest of the Keepers, she took out her phone and dialed the police. They protected her as she then played dead.

Crazy T was too focused on his prize to notice or care, for just then, Zipper had turned and faced Mrs. Walters as well as Tom's and Alex's brothers. The young men were fighting to get across the field to their wounded siblings. It was clear what Crazy T was having Zipper do. He was using Tom and Alex as bait so that Crazy T could finish the job he started over a decade ago. The storm now raged in full. The brothers, along with some concerned parents, slid in the mud and hail as they ran after their siblings and children. Zipper shot every last one.

The sight infuriated me. Kyla sent a bolt my way, but I had grown too full of fury to be subject to her depression and rage. I held my hand out and grabbed the bolt she sent flying at me. She sent another. I grabbed it, then flew, like some samurai from an old movie, towards her, shrieking in the way only a Taker can. I cut her ghostly form to pieces with both bolts until what was left of Kyla, her mass of mist, came apart, sucked into The Flow.

"Fay," Kyla said in her final moments.

I felt her presence again. For a moment, she was herself, the drinking buddy I knew before the crash, the girl I grew up with, who let me kiss Alex first.

Her eyes were so bright, so green at that moment.

"I'm sorry, Kyla, but you made your choice," I said. "There's nothing I can do."

Just then, The Flow sucked her shrieking ghostly form, all misty, red and black, inside. I turned away, fearful of what it might look like to see a close friend go to hell.

I didn't let the crying on the field—that of older adults, of children, of teenagers—get to me.

I marched towards Zipper, determined to do whatever was needed to take him out.

Crazy T enjoyed himself, gazing as he did over all the carnage. The blood only acted like an upper. A twisted smile crossed Zipper's lips as Crazy T set eyes on Mrs. Walters, the good teacher, there alone, fighting to protect a few of the kids with her own body. She was visibly shaking, struggling to be brave.

"How sweet," Zipper said. "Where was that sweetness when I needed it, when Steve tormented me?!"

Mrs. Walters made eye contact with Zipper. "What did you say?" she asked.

"I loved you," Zipper said. "I only ever loved *you*!"

"No," Mrs. Walters said weakly, fearful of having started two shootings and not just one. "Zipper, whatever that is, it's not healthy, it's not love. Put the gun down. Let me get you some help."

"I loved you so much, just like this freak loved Fay; more, even more," Zipper told her. "How can you say I never loved you?"

Crazy T used Zipper's hand to stroke the cheek of his beloved.

Mrs. Walters looked carefully into the eyes of her assailant.

"Teddy?" she asked.

Zipper raised the gun in a token of greeting. "Ready to go to hell with me?" he asked. "We mustn't keep your friends waiting."

Zipper pointed the gun. Mrs. Walters screamed. She tried so hard to be brave, even if she was not naturally a brave woman. The children she protected screamed with her.

The exchange between Mrs. Walters and Crazy T bought me the moment I needed. I tried to slip into Steph, but she wouldn't let me. I used my Taker rage, convincing her to come from where she was cowering and stand up to Zipper.

I felt her strength, her outrage, her trauma. I joined it to mine.

She rose.

In the split second that Steph used to get across the field, Zipper prepared to pull the trigger.

Just then, Mandy, close enough to hear the exchange, flipped her wheelchair over. The sound of the crashing chair caught Zipper's attention. Crazy T screamed at Zipper to shoot, but the sight of the crippled crash victim on the ground moved something in Zipper, and he did not turn away. Mandy took advantage of the moment and yelled, "Fay said to save her a dance! I saw her. I swear it!"

Zipper halted. "What did you say?" he asked.

In that one second, Mandy saved Mrs. Walters' life.

"Don't," Steph screamed at Zipper as she came closer.

Her knees buckled; she lost her will. I joined my spirit with hers to give her strength.

"Enough death," Steph screamed. "We've lost enough!"

"Get out of the girl," Crazy T called to me.

"Not until you leave Zipper," I said.

"To think," Zipper said to Steph. "I *might* have let you live. But you clearly haven't suffered enough."

I radiated in my black mist as best I could until Zipper could see me.

There I was, a dark ghost, nearly as shadowy as Kyla, who was now gone to hell.

Zipper's eyes reddened. "Fay?" he asked.

"I won't let you kill her," I said through Steph. "I took her mother. I won't let you take her. And I won't let Crazy T take Mrs. Walters."

"Crazy who?"

"There's no time," I said to Zipper. "You have to listen to me."

"What?"

My eyes made it to a few of the wounded soccer players on the field. They were going to make one last strike against Zipper. Their eyes showed more ferocity at that moment than they had in their entire championship season. They had a field to cross, but they would get there.

"You set me up," Zipper said. "I loved you, Fay, and all you could do was try to trick me."

"No one can trick you now," I told Zipper. "They're getting closer. You have a choice to make."

"What choice?"

"I'm here for you. I'm your Taker."

"What?"

"I've always been your Taker. I died so that you would do this, so that you would be manipulated into doing this. I'm trying to set things right."

"I gave them what they deserved!" Zipper shouted. He looked right into the eyes of the soccer players pressing closer to him as he said: "They killed you! They made you a drunk!"

I touched Zipper's face in an attempt at compassion.

"*I* made the decision to drink alcohol," I said. "*I* made the choice to get behind the wheel. I may not have chosen to be an alcoholic, but *I* chose to ignore my disease and look what happened."

Zipper looked uncertain.

"What I did was my fault and no one else's," I told him. "What you did was your fault, too."

Zipper began to cry.

"I care about you, Zipper," I said, "but I care about them too. I won't let you kill any more of them."

"Fay?" Zipper asked.

He was such a helpless little boy. The full magnitude of what he did was beginning to seize him. He sobbed, still holding his assault rifle, but still fearful.

The soccer team was stumbling over bodies, but picking up momentum.

"Feels awful, doesn't it?" I asked Zipper. "I know how that feels. I feel it every moment after taking Steph's mom away from her, after crippling Mandy, after contributing to the death of Kyla. But they made their choices that night, too, Zipper, just as you made your choice now. Just as you have to make a choice this very second."

Zipper's light showed the faint glow of understanding.

The very second what was left of the soccer team got near him, Zipper pointed his gun at them. His eyes grew opaque, unreadable. He muttered only, "I'm sorry...I'm so sorry that I was ever born."

He then aimed the gun point blank at his own skull and shot.

The soccer players tackled Zipper, but it was too late. His lifeless body went down without a fight.

I released Steph, who stood there, aware of what I'd said and done, but uncertain of how to feel.

"She protected me," she whispered to herself. "*She,* of all people, protected *me.*"

Before Steph lost the feel of my soul entirely, I sent her one last message.

"Alex loves you," I told her. "Just as I love him. Be the girlfriend to him that I never was. Don't mess it up."

"Fay?" a ghostly voice called. "Your head? Where is your beautiful head?"

It was Zipper, in his new form. He looked like he was a shadow engulfed in fire.

"Gone," I said. "Decapitated."

The Flow crackled in anticipation of more souls. Crazy T lunged to take Zipper, to take as many souls as he could down with him, but the darkness of his deeds was too much. Crazy T got his wish. The Flow sucked him in, screaming as he was, and swallowed him straight to hell, along with nearly every Taker that raised a ghostly hand in the fight. Even the Keepers were sucked in, though their vortex led to a far better place. I saw Belinda stand next to me for a moment. The Flow called to her.

"Belinda?" Zipper asked. "From elementary school?"

Belinda nodded and then turned to me.

"I wanted to say goodbye the right way this time," Belinda said to me. "The way we should've in the hospital when we were young."

I hugged her. A part of her golden light, if just for a moment, filled me.

"Thank you," I said.

Belinda's glow diminished ever so slightly.

"We lost many," Belinda said. "I wish I'd done better."

"The bombs didn't all detonate because of you," I said.

"And because of my sisters and brothers," she said. "We all played a role, even you. And I promise you: Our energy will keep the bombs from exploding when the bomb squads clear them out."

"Thank you," I said.

Belinda smiled. Her radiance returned to a blinding white light.

"Off to heaven?" I asked her.

"I can only hope."

"I'm never going, am I?" I asked.

"That remains to be seen," she said. "Takers don't all go to hell. They aren't all evil. Just the leaders like Crazy T who can't let go, who twist others to their will."

"I'll remember that."

"Good," Belinda said. "You're their leader now, you know that? The most powerful Taker still left. You lived a rotten life. Live a better after-life."

"I will."

I looked around; it wasn't just Zipper gravitating towards me. The souls of other students, some soccer players, who died without fully embracing the light, hovered near me too.

"Can they see heaven—through your eyes?" I asked. "Can they see it just once so that they know?"

"Everyone sees heaven differently," Belinda told me. "But I have a feeling many of them will see it one day, when their work here is done."

Belinda turned to my fellow Takers and to me. "Just never forget the light inside you," she said, "no matter how dark it gets around you."

Belinda waved, and just like that The Flow swallowed her into a haven of pure light.

"Goodbye, my friend," I whispered.

"Where are we?" a dead soccer player asked.

His form was that of a dark, shapeless mist with bullets circling it.

I looked at Zipper, at the soccer player, at the kid just out for a night of fun.

"We're where we need to be, somewhere between heaven, hell, and earth. We're Takers."

"What are those?"

"You'll see."

Just then, ambulances and police cars arrived. I'd experienced this scene before. I walked with my fellow Takers, seizing any last lost souls among the number of bodies. I watched as the bodies were rounded up, as the wounded, like Alex, received their care. Tourniquets were everywhere, as was the blood. Stretchers moved countless kids to more ambulances than I'd ever seen gathered in a single place. The number of wounded was truly staggering.

In the midst of all of this, Mandy embraced Steph as she circled around.

"I'm sorry," Mandy said. "I'm so sorry."

"I know," Steph said, hugging her back. "I can't forgive you yet, but I'll get there."

Just then, Alex came up, newly bandaged, and held Steph. She held him back.

"It's time for us to go," I said to my new Takers.

"Go where?" Zipper asked.

"Spree."

"What's that?"

"It's where Takers take souls."

"Why?"

"Judgment...and penance."

Zipper cried. "There is no penance for me," he said. "I deserve to go to hell."

"Leave the judgment to Spree, but remember," I said, facing all the new Takers, "you each get one wish. A Death Day wish. Choose wisely, especially if you think hell follows."

"I choose for you to go to heaven," Zipper told me.

None too surprisingly, the prayers of murderers weren't that powerful. I was still there.

"It's okay. I belong here," I said.

"Why?"

"To clean up what I've done," I said. "I hope you spend more time here than me. You need to learn how to be human again."

"As a ghost?"

"How else?"

I hugged Mandy and stood with my friends until every last person was cleared from the field.

How dark the muddy field looked, all stained with blood.

As if it was a sign from God, we set our eyes on the field and disappeared.

Zipper's Death Day wish sent us straight to Spree, straight home.

MONTHS LATER

CHAPTER 13

The Burgundy Hill High School Memorial game may not have been a sanctioned championship soccer match, but it showed that Burgundy Hill was, much like the game of soccer itself, resilient and full of character. The game was held well after the original game to accommodate the bomb squads. It's sad that the term would ever have to be associated with schools, but it was. Naturally, classes weren't held until the school was thoroughly combed and every last bomb and piece of metal was cleaned out. It took weeks. Some parents still felt uncomfortable, and it's rumored Burgundy Hill Prepatory Academy had a big spike in mid-year enrollment because of it.

"I can feel their pain," Zipper said. "It burns me."

His lasting ghostly form was that of a scarecrow in perpetual fire. Each day, the weight of what he had done grew in the fires upon him.

"You haven't felt nearly any of it yet," I said. "But you will. Just as I'll always feel the emptiness I created in Steph's soul."

I worried about Zipper, strange as he was. He grew darker by the day, twisted and distorted by the pain. He could feel the hatred of the community, and that twisted him further.

I imagined in another few months he'd be gone, swallowed up by hell. I'd have to help him, somehow.

As he stood by me, though, I wanted him to see the moment of his defeat, the moment of Burgundy Hill's triumph.

The crowning moment before the game was the dedication of the Tree of Life, as the Vocational Agricultural sponsors called it. It was the sapling of a giant elm tree planted that spring that would symbolize the connection with nature every lost life had. The entire school came out one day to see the commemorating of the tree and the game they never had a chance to see earlier on. It was the only year there wasn't one state champion, and a year when both Burgundy Hill and Franklin Shore were honored with championship trophies. Still, both teams were rivals and athletes and wanted to know who the better team was. Even if it meant playing without some of their best players.

In the stands, on cell phones, I saw the latest on The Burgundy Hill Slayings. We now had our own Wikipedia page, complete with a picture of John "Zipper" Chatterly and most of the soccer players. I was an addendum on the page, the supposed motive for the trigger man. And it wasn't just Wikipedia who gave us that dubious honor. It was countless Facebook walls, Twitter feeds, and additions to the long list of school shootings that websites updated by the year. The very web page Zipper studied only months ago now added him to the list.

I showed the Wiki page to Zipper.

"Can you believe I wanted this?" he asked. The page was covered with his supernatural blood. "Now, it only gives me pain."

"For every soul who looks upon that page, your fire will burn brighter. So says the council of Spree."

"Until it extinguishes me?" Zipper asked. "Until I just die?"

"Not this fire," I told him. "It never completely burns itself out."

I stood by Zipper, watching his punishment in what seemed a few moments, though it took place over weeks in the mortal world.

Cameras circled Burgundy Hill tenaciously. Reporters were everywhere, addressing everything from motive to the school's safety issues, to bomb removal, to the recovery of the soccer team. There was even a rumor that a TV movie was in the works, one making heroes of the soccer team that fought to bring down a shooter. It was originally slated for wide-screen release, but studio executives feared high schoolers would rather see made-up horror movies with ghosts and vampires. One screenplay even had me star as a ghost looking in on what my drunk driving accident had caused, but the script was deemed too insensitive to the Burgundy Hill disasters of the year and ultimately passed on.

"Tell me, before I go to hell," Zipper said. "Will they ever make a movie of this?"

"A low budget one, and you'll be portrayed as a monster."

"If only I saw all this before, it could've been avoided," Zipper said.

I looked sternly at him, speaking as his Taker: "Nothing would've changed your mind once I'd died. I'm so sorry, John. I should've been a better person to you. We all had a hand in what led up to this disaster."

"But I was sick in the head."

"You were sick in the soul; for that there is no cure...short of Jesus."

The fire ignited again—some new view on the Wikipedia page, perhaps, some new mention of his name.

I looked at Zipper and shook my head.

What saddened me was that this wasn't the way any town wants to be remembered. I never wanted to be known as the drunk girl who got decapitated, and Burgundy Hill never wanted to be known as the center of a school shooting. Neither did Columbine. But here we both were, hot media stories until the next shooting happened and the next group of administrators, counselors, and teachers got grilled for not recognizing the warning signs. The truth is, until it happens, nobody really thinks the kid next to her, no matter how deranged, is going to bring in a gun and blow half the school away.

It's unnatural, but it keeps happening, throughout time.

Our case did have one point of distinction, however, to forever grace our web pages. The press portrayed Zipper as a somewhat popular kid rather than the gun-toting loner I remembered him as. There were no trench coats, no bad home relationships. Even Zipper's bullying at the hands of the soccer team went undiscovered. His blog, while cryptic, gave no insight. Ironically, Zipper actually lent his nickname to the type of school shooter who showed few signs, integrated well with others, and managed to avoid detection. Sort of like the Trench Coat Mafia, he became engrained into the pop culture of the moment. Then, he was forgotten.

"Will anyone remember me as I was before the killing?" Zipper's ghost asked me.

"I'll try," I told him. "But even I can never forget what you did, just as no one can forget what I did."

I winced in a pain of my own.

The reason: my mother, too, made the news. The headline: "Mother of Drunk Driver Loses House."

Mandy's family's lawsuit, like Steph's family's suit, went all the way to court. To pay the court-ordered amount, my mother sold the house. She told reporters: "It wasn't a home anymore without Fay."

But I knew she loved that house. I'd cost her that much, on top of giving her an empty home.

The community paper, *The Burgundy Hill Observer,* ran articles asking for financial and emotional support for all the families of the victims, and my mother and her plight were printed with her blessing.

Still, no one feels sorry for the mother of a drunk driver when there were innocent kids gunned down. Some even blamed her for the way I turned out. But looking into the timeline, I knew I would've gotten behind that wheel no matter what. I was an alcoholic and unless I admitted it and asked for help, the story would've ended the same way—just later in life, after I had kids of my own.

For those of my friends whose story did end, and it was a long list, most became Keepers.

Two starters for Westfield, including Will Coldon, ended up Keepers.

At least five members of each team were dead. I only saw two players, a kid named Ben, and Tom, who became a Taker in training.

While Jessica survived, Sue was also here, but so dark in form I barely recognized her.

One baby was killed.

Her soul was so precious and so beautiful it became a blinding white light that rose straight to heaven.

Two small kids died. They became angels of light, too.

Both Coach Ryan and Coach Derriza died.

I can only hope they went to heaven.

So many died.

So many I never saw again.

They were remembered only in the hearts of those who knew them.

But there was one ray of heavenly light.

Alex lived, and he and Steph began the relationship that would lead to their marriage.

How I envied Steph, but how I knew this was the medicine of the soul that she needed: love, pure, unconditional, love, if only a shadow of the mother's love that I'd taken away from her.

One day, I'd meet up with Steph's mother again. One day, I'd ask her if I did well saving her daughter's life, if I'd kept my word.

I can only imagine that, after all this, she'd smile.

Even Takers have dreams; that was mine.

But now it was time for reality, and so my attention drifted back to the game.

The plays were a pale imitation of the hard-hitting action that started off the championship game, but the game wasn't in the plays. It was in the smiles of the boys who played like teenagers should, having the time of their lives, laughing again, as they jousted back and forth across a field no longer drenched in blood, but blossoming in a life not even the massacre of late fall could kill. Suddenly, a bright light took the field. I felt the ghosts of the other players, who for a brief moment, joined them from Spree, playing the game in the field, each side knowing, so assuredly, that Burgundy Hill would win, that Franklin Shore would win, that they'd have the game of their lives.

In the final seconds of the exhibition, which Burgundy Hill did win 3-2, I saw a sight I thought my ghostly eyes would never see again.

There, joining the spectators, surrounded by the other Burgundy Hill mothers, was my mom.

She'd been working hard to make the court payments, renting a tiny apartment on the edge of town. But here she was, clapping for the boys, calling out for them, along with the other Burgundy Hill mothers.

This was the way soccer was meant to be.

This was the way our senior year should have been all along.

LATE JUNE

CHAPTER 14

Taking souls became second nature to me, but I never tormented a single soul the way Crazy T did me. I didn't manipulate their fates for my own personal gain. I simply led them to Spree, where they became a Keeper, Taker, or went straight to heaven or hell. I'd even seen heaven in small glimpses—for me, it was just an ocean of light stemming from a long, white-sanded and silt-shored river. There was a tremendous feeling of peace, of a sobriety that wasn't painful to achieve. But the vision always came to an end a split second later as the soul I ushered turned back and waved and was gone. At least I knew there was a God. Maybe one day I'd see Him for myself.

I never thought I'd see any of my old friends again after the shooting.

Even Zipper became darker and eventually broke away. I fought to bring him memories of light, but the darkness surrounding him was so vast. Other Takers said they saw hell swallow him. As his Taker, I felt it, even though I wasn't there.

I was here, in the middle of what should have been my graduation ceremony, looking on.

How serious my friends all looked. Chairs were decorated with robes, a diploma, and flowers for those of us who didn't make it to the end. An entire front row of seats was set aside, for myself, for Kyla, for Tom, for Sue, for all those lives lost, too many for such a young class. I was tempted to sit in my seat—Sue actually did sit in hers—to feel what graduation would be like, but I knew that what Belinda said during that battle months ago was just as true today. Fay was dead. The Taker was what remained.

Moments before the conferring of the diplomas, my school had a special speaker approach the podium. I'd been so busy working as a Taker that I hadn't taken the time to feel the aura of my mother in months, and I was stunned. She was dressed not in a business suit, but in a simple pink and white dress. She was dressed as Mom.

"I'm not a speaker like your congressman is. Most of you know me. I'm Mrs. DeSoto. Fay was my daughter."

The entire audience grew silent. For an outdoor graduation, with each seat full, that was saying something.

"Today I don't just speak as a mother, but as a Burgundy Hill mother, about what it was like to wake up and find out that my daughter had died and killed two other people," Mom began. "I want to speak about what it was like to wake up and find that a school shooting had happened, that my daughter's death was believed to be part of the motive. I want to speak of those things, but I'm just a mom, and I can't find the words. All I can say is that my heart never left the night of November 3rd. And I bet yours never left another November night, only days later. But, together, you made it here today. The first thing I'd ask you to do is to not forget my daughter or the friends you lost on the night of the shooting. Talk about them. Keep them alive. Just don't dwell on them. Give them a hug like you would any friend you're about to say goodbye to. And remember the laughter, the joy, the blessing from God that each of them was in our lives."

Mom grew emotional here; the crowd kept quiet.

"I'm not going to take time away from your speakers," Mom said, "but I just want to ask you not to let a moment of your life be wasted. Live for Fay, for Tom, for Lynn, who you knew as Steph's mother, for every friend you had to say goodbye to far too soon. Just live. Don't let their deaths be yours. Don't let the fact that you're the only class in Burgundy Hill history to graduate so close to July stop you. Don't let yourself be labeled the dysfunctional class, the class of the shooting. Aren't your smiles, your nights out, your friendships worth more than that? Tragedy shapes us, that's true. But it needn't define us, not everything that we are. Smiles shape us too. Don't let a day go by without smiling for the lives we honor here today."

Mom paused, fighting to regain her focus.

"Let me just end by saying that the night of November 3rd I opened the door to have two police officers tell me that my daughter was dead. I then shut the door and kept it shut. Today, June 30th, I'm opening that door, even if it is to a smaller place than the place I lived in then. I'm letting life back in. You see, Fay's never coming home. She drank. She made a bad choice. Some of your friends are never coming home. They protected us with their lives. They made a good choice. No, none of them are ever coming home, but for the best of reasons: They are home already. They're home in our hearts. I beg you: Don't be like I was. Open the door to each other, not just to classmates, not just to friends, but to family because family is forever and every one of you is family now. Turn to the person next to you. Hug them. Call them brother. Call them sister. We are all family now."

Mom left the podium. The audience was silent for a moment, a long, staggered moment, absorbing her brief words. Just then, a tidal wave of cheers, of hugs, of applause went up. Up and down the rows, graduates were hugging people they'd hardly known just seven months ago, people who were closer to them than some of their relatives were now.

As Mom left, I caught a glimpse of the state congressman who was to follow that speech. I'm sure his words would be more articulate, his delivery better rehearsed, but I'd never want to be him. I knew no words were more powerful than the words that came from the bottom of a mother's heart.

I applauded, joined in the cheering, the hugging, even if I was unseen.

Sue did too. We even hugged each other briefly.

Just then, I heard a tiny, sweet voice. I heard Belinda.

"Fancy seeing you here," she said.

She looked like a bright white angel, wings and all.

"I felt pulled here," I told her.

"So did I, by the strength of a mother's love," Belinda said.

The head I held in my arms shook in denial. "I'm sorry, but that's not the reason I'm here."

"You're kidding."

I said nothing.

Kids started walking across the stage. I saw Alex, limping, make it. I saw Steph with the first smile I'd seen on her face in quite some time. I heard my name called, to applause I didn't deserve. But the biggest applause went to Mandy, who wheeled her way across the stage with undeniable grace. She'd buckled down in her studies and was granted late acceptance to a second tier Ivy League school. I was so proud of her. I was so proud of them all.

Except one.

"How in the world will this kid die?" Belinda asked.

"How did I die?"

"Another drunk driver? After all they just heard?" she asked. "After what happened to you? After a school shooting?"

"Don't ask me," I said. "I'm just the Taker."

"Can't you stop it?"

"Of course I'll try, but—"

"But the kid's mind is already made up."

"To party way too much, yes," I said.

Belinda watched as the class turned their tassels, tossed their caps up in the air.

"But which one?" she asked.

I scanned the crowd. "I won't know until it's time. It could be anyone," I said. "I was just another kid several months ago."

Kids marched down, following the heads of their rows, to the waiting arms of their families. I followed the graduates, saying my goodbyes to Belinda.

Later that night, another mom in the audience would get the call.

Later that night, another Taker would be born.

www.ingramcontent.com/pod-product-compliance
Lightning Source LLC
Chambersburg PA
CBHW020956180626
46814CB00003B/1122